The Murder of Vincent Dunn

By Tom MacDonald

Other Dermot Sparhawk Novels by Tom MacDonald

The Charlestown Connection

Beyond the Bridge

The Revenge of Liam McGrew

Murder in the Charlestown Bricks

ISBN: 978-0-9967332-5-0

Printed in U.S.A.

In memory of my aunt and godmother
Cathleen Conley
She brought joy wherever she went

For three dear friends
I lost this past year . . .

Maura (O'Grady) Wilkins
County Sligo, Ireland
Milton Highlanders

Jack "Jazz" Flemming
South Boston, Mass.
Braintree S.O.S.

Bob Rooney
Charlestown, Mass.
St. Vincent DePaul Society

1

THE 6:00 A.M. phone call surprised me, and so did the man calling, a New Hampshire state police captain named Leo Raymond. He asked if I was Dermot Sparhawk of Louis & Sparhawk Law and Investigations in Charlestown. I told him I was. Raymond said he wanted to hire me to look into a matter that he, because of circumstances in the state police, couldn't investigate himself. Before we talked about the issue at hand, I asked him how he got my name. He told me he got it from a Boston police superintendent named Dennis Hanson. He went on to say that Hanson had highly recommended me for the job. *Hanson recommended me?* Must be a blue moon.

"What can I do for you, Captain?" I asked him.

"I'd rather discuss it in person," he said.

I was between cases at the moment and itching for something to do. I told Raymond we could meet in my Boston office at his earliest convenience.

"Not Boston," he said.

"I can shoot up to New Hampshire, no problem."

"Not New Hampshire, either," he said, sounding somewhat guarded. "I'd rather meet in Lowell if that's possible."

"Lowell, it is."

"Today works best for me, Mr. Sparhawk. I will of course reimburse you for your travel expenses. Is today okay for you?"

"Today is fine," I said. "Where in Lowell?"

"McDermott's Green," he answered.

How did he know about McDermott's Green? I thought it was a family nickname for a patch of grass next to a church.

He asked me if I knew where it was, "because McDermott's Green won't show up on your GPS." I told him I knew where it was. I knew the story behind the naming of it, too. Red McDermott, a smalltime bookie who refused to pay tribute to the Somerville mob, was murdered in a Lowell neighborhood called the Acre. Red was my father's friend. They served together in Vietnam as Marines, boonie rats in the boondocks, my father told me.

I remembered the day my father took me to Red's funeral Mass. I was thirteen, and much to my surprise I was allowed to skip school to attend the service. My father introduced me to the world of workingmen that day, to their black-and-white outlook and their tough banter. Their gruffness masked the love they had for each other, a love they couldn't convey directly, so they conveyed it with humor and putdowns. It worked.

After the Mass, Red's widow scattered his ashes on what is casually known as McDermott's Green. I remembered that it was a windy day and the ashes blew everywhere. The priest who celebrated the funeral pretended not to see the scattering. The Catholic Church requires that the dead, even in the form of ashes, be buried in consecrated ground--*probably because they own so many cemeteries.*

After the ceremony we ate at a Greek restaurant on Market Street. It was a somber occasion and the last memory I have of my father. He died the next day at work, tripping off a length of scaffolding while washing windows on a Back Bay high-rise on Boylston Street. The window-washing gig was a stop-gap, something to tide him over after he drank his way off the ironworkers. He fell ten stories to the sidewalk below. The police called it a clean landing. He missed the lunchtime pedestrians.

At the wake his boss assured me my father wasn't drunk, 'So don't worry about the life insurance payout,' a pittance that went

"That was a lifetime ago." I looked down and kicked a pebble. "Another lifetime."

"It wasn't *that* long ago." He pursued it. "You were twice named All-American, you won the Butkus Award, and you were a finalist for the Heisman Trophy." Raymond sounded like a press secretary for a college athletic department. He wasn't finished. "The pro scouts had you going high in the first round." He removed his Red Sox cap and finger combed his silver hair. "That knee injury was a rotten break, just horrible. You'd have been a great pro if you didn't blow out that knee."

He was right about that. The knee injury torpedoed my dreams and led to drinking. The drinking torpedoed my life and led to restraints in a locked ward. Time to change the subject.

"Thanks, Captain." I cleared my throat. "Why did you want to meet today?"

Raymond refitted the Sox cap on his head and stood straighter if that was possible.

"We found a body floating in the Nashua River." He watched a Lowell Parks Department truck go by. "The victim's name was Vincent Dunn. He was dumped in the water, after he was shot in the mouth and head."

"Sounds gruesome," I said. "Why call me?"

"Dunn was from Charlestown."

"Vincent Dunn," I repeated the name.

"Did you know him?" he asked.

The Vincent Dunn I knew supposedly beat a man to death with a hammer in a backroom poker game. The alleged incident took place about twenty years ago when I was a kid, right around the time of Red McDermott's funeral and my father's fall from the scaffolding.

As I remembered it, the victim's body was never found. Townies began to wonder if the story was a hoax, another urban myth attributed to a neighborhood built on urban myths. Nobody came forward to testify, but you'd expect that in Charlestown. No evidence, no body, no charges were brought. Vincent Dunn skated. He continued his life of crime and now he's dead. Maybe fate caught up to him.

"I know *of* him," I said. "I heard he went away for armed robbery a while ago."

"He did go away." Raymond confirmed. "Dunn served eight years inside a federal pen in Pennsylvania. He was paroled last month, early release for good behavior."

"A Townie getting out for good behavior? How did that happen?"

"Earned time off," he said, answering my smart-ass question. "Dunn went to Alcoholics Anonymous meetings and anger-management counseling. He completed a recidivism course."

"A what?"

"A course that helps repeat offenders stop repeating."

"Did he pass?"

He ignored me.

"But most importantly, the warden liked him." Raymond hitched his thumbs in the belt loops. "I got to know Dunn at a soup kitchen in Nashua. We volunteered serving lunch."

Charitable of Vincent. "What else can you tell me about him?"

"Dunn was doing everything right. He sobered up, cleaned up, and landed a job. He was giving back to the community. And after all that, after all the positive steps he took to put his life right, he gets murdered. I think he deserves justice."

A cop who thinks a crook deserves justice? Vincent Dunn must have impressed the hell out of Captain Raymond.

"I'm all for justice." I wanted to work on this thing. "Dunn deserves justice."

"I'm glad you feel that way."

"You said he was shot in the head."

"Two times," Raymond said. "Once in the mouth, once in the ear."

"Sounds to me like *someone* was angry at him."

"It wasn't random in my opinion."

I looked at the fading grass on McDermott's Green. The

surrounding oaks and elms were bare of leaves, and the exposed branches were knobby and gray. A lone seagull flew off the church steeple and headed for downtown Lowell, soaring above a blue-gray skyline of brick smokestacks and repurposed mill buildings. The gull dove low toward the standing canals and crumbling railroad beds. Lowell, America's first rustbelt city.

"Where do I come in?" I asked.

"I'll get to that in a second," he said. "A Nashua police detective named Remy Vachon is leading the investigation. Vachon knows the city of Nashua and everyone in it. He was also the first one at the scene. Vachon is in charge."

"Is he good?"

"Damn good," he said. "Nashua has one of the best police departments in the country. They are professional and squared away. Vachon reflects that excellence."

Raymond should write obituaries the way he pumps people up.

"Nashua is handling the murder case, not the state police?" I asked.

"Nashua is heading it," he said. "Why?"

"In Massachusetts the state police investigate homicides outside of Boston." I studied Raymond's face, trying to figure him out. "Are you working with Detective Vachon as a liaison or something?"

"My colonel said no." Raymond looked up. "I'm retiring next month. The colonel didn't want me to start a new investigation."

"That makes sense."

"Not to me it doesn't," he said. "I can outwork and outthink every cop investigating the murder, including Vachon. But none of that matters now. I'm out in a month."

"You're retiring."

"I was forced out, but that's a story for another day," he said. "I called you today because I want to make sure the Dunn case is done right, that it gets the full attention it deserves. I want you to look into it and report back to me, and only to me."

"A shadow investigation?" I laughed. "You're kidding, right?"

"I never kid about homicide," he said. "I considered Vincent Dunn a friend, and as a friend, I want his case to get the full attention it deserves."

"You don't trust the Nashua police to handle it themselves? You just said they were an excellent department."

"I want a second pair of eyes on it," he said, evading the question. "The truth is I want someone from Charlestown."

"What about Detective Vachon?"

"There is no reason to tell him about your involvement," he said. "He'll do his thing, we'll do ours."

"Come on, Captain. Vachon will find out." Even I knew that much. "And when he does, he'll have me drawn and quartered by the mounted division."

"I thought private detectives made a living bucking authority," Raymond said. "What are you afraid of?"

"Plenty," I said. "Interfering with a police investigation doesn't seem very smart to me, especially when the police department is in another state."

"I'll grant you it could get nasty."

I didn't want Raymond to withdraw the offer.

"On the other hand, investigating a Townie's murder stirs my adrenaline."

"Does that mean you'll take the job?"

"I'll take the job," I said.

"I was hoping you'd say that." Raymond handed me an envelope. "Inside you will find a temporary New Hampshire private investigator's license. It's valid for three months. Take this, too." He gave me a thick folder bound by a rubber band. "The initial crime report from Detective Remy Vachon. It's all in there. Forensics, photos, witness statements, everything you'll need to get started. You'll find a retainer of twenty-five hundred dollars in there, too."

"You were pretty confident I'd take the case."

"Your reputation precedes you." He reached into his pocket. "Here's my card. Call me if you need anything. I'd appreciate weekly updates."

"I'll call when I have something to report," I said, managing Raymond's expectations. "I'm curious about something. Why did you pick McDermott's Green to meet?"

"I'm in Lowell today on business, attending a meeting up the street." He pointed in the direction of downtown. "I can walk to it from here."

"That's not what I meant. What I meant was—"

"Sorry to cut you short, Dermot, but I have to run. The meeting starts in ten minutes."

He shook my hand and walked away.

Why didn't he say St. Patrick Church instead of McDermott's Green? St. Patrick's would show up on a GPS search. Something didn't feel right about the way he handled the question. Maybe I was making a big deal out of nothing. I went back to my car with a job to do.

3

FROM MCDERMOTT'S GREEN I drove to Athenian Corner, where my father and I ate our last meal together after Red's funeral. I've been going to the Athenian once a month since the day I got my driver's license. I go to keep alive the memory of my father, and to keep alive my taste buds. The food is the best.

I ordered chicken kabobs with green beans and rice, a bowl of lentil soup, and a Greek salad. The always friendly waitress, Thea, jotted it down and went to the kitchen. After eating the meal and unearthing a burp, I toiled through the police report. The tedium of reading cop-prose was eased when Thea delivered a dish of baklava with vanilla ice cream and gooey sauce, courtesy of her father and owner, Stavros, the Greek immigrant who founded the place. I nodded my thanks and ate a spoonful. A sugar high, the best medicine for a recovering alcoholic.

I flipped to the next page. On October 23rd at three in the afternoon, a woman named Claire Corneau was walking her dog on Canal Street when she saw a body floating in the Nashua River and called 911. The next witness, a man named Leonard Rancourt, also saw the body. He too called the police. I wrote their contact info in my notepad. I doubted I'd follow up with them.

The Nashua Police Department responded to the calls and fished Vincent Dunn out of the marshy weeds at four o'clock.

Detective Remy Vachon signed the report. I looked at the crime photos of Dunn, with his face shot and bruised and his hair wet and slicked back. I looked at his mugshot from eight years ago, when he was convicted of armed robbery. No one ever smiles in mugshots. I thought I recognized him, but I could be imaging it, the result of seeing too many Irish-faced Townies in too many mugshots over too many years.

I closed the folder and called Buckley Louis, my partner in Louis & Sparhawk, and told him about my meeting with Captain Leo Raymond at McDermott's Green. Buckley grumbled and asked me a battery of questions. I did my best to answer them, but he's a lawyer and he came at me fast. I felt like a chump on a witness stand. Buckley asked more questions, questions that carried an accusatory tone.

"Raymond hired you to investigate Vincent Dunn's murder," Buckley said. "I don't like it, Dermot. Cops don't hire private investigators to solve murders, not when there's an ongoing investigation. It sounds like a setup to me."

"I thought the same thing, but I liked Raymond. I liked that he wanted to get justice for Vincent Dunn. My instincts are telling me it's not a setup."

"Your instincts again." He sighed. "You and your Micmac instincts."

"I'm not stupid, Buck. Raymond is holding something back. I found it strange that he wanted to meet in Lowell instead of at our office. He must have had his reasons."

"Yeah, but what are his reasons? What is he up to?"

"He wants to get justice for Dunn," I said. "That's all there is to it."

"Un-uh, no way," he said. "*My* instincts are telling me there's more to it."

"There's always more to it. You know that."

"So you're moving ahead with the case."

"That's what I've been saying."

"Hmm." Buckley always says hmm when he's mulling a problem. "I'd feel much better about it if Harraseeket Kid was working with you. When does he get back from Nova Scotia?"

"Don't know," I said. "I'll call him when I get off the phone with you."

"Make sure you do."

It felt good to be doing something again.

4

IN NASHUA I booked a room at Henri's Motor Lodge, a shoddy motel with paper-thin walls located next to an exit ramp on Route 3. The racket reminded me of the Tobin Bridge. I soon fell asleep. At five in the morning someone with a heavy hand banged on the door. I opened it, expecting to see a knuckle-dragger with a plunger telling me the pipes were clogged. I was wrong. It was Harraseeket Kid, dressed in denim jeans and a black Dropkick Murphys hoody. He was carrying two cups of coffee, thank God, and he handed one to me.

"Hey, Sleeping Beauty, you're missing half the day."

I grunted and let the steam warm my nostrils.

Harraseeket Kid is my first cousin and a full-blooded Micmac Indian. He wears his black hair in a long ponytail to honor his heritage. He is big and tough, smart and strong, and usually armed with a knife and a gun. Nobody messes with Kid, which comes in handy in my line of work. He sat in a chair and plunked his cowboy boots on the coffee table.

"Buck filled me in," he said. "Tell me the plan."

"I don't have a plan yet." I told him. "Let's put our heads together and see what we come up with."

"Sounds good."

And after an exhaustive two-minute brainstorming session, we came up with a plan. Kid would follow Detective Vachon of the Nashua police, and I would investigate Vincent Dunn of the Nashua River. We agreed to meet back at Henri's Motor Lodge at seven o'clock tonight.

Outside in the parking lot Kid opened the door to his bright red Ford Super Duty F-450 and stepped onto the running board to vault in. The truck had chrome mags, chrome mudguards, a chrome air horn, and a diamond-plated bed cover. A clanging firetruck was less conspicuous.

"Let's switch vehicles," I said. "A police detective *might* notice you following him in that fluorescent tank of yours. It practically glows in the dark."

"Pissa, and I'm stuck with your sissy car?" He tossed me the keys. "Don't dent it. I just waxed her yesterday."

"I'll do my best to avoid mud puddles."

"You'd better."

I got into the truck and opened my briefcase. According to the police report, Vincent Dunn had been working at McNally's Tap at the time of his death. Dunn was working in a bar? Captain Raymond told me that Dunn went to AA meetings in prison, so why was he working in a bar? I couldn't do it. Too much temptation. I typed McNally's Tap into the GPS. It was located on Canal Street near the Nashua River. I drove there in Kid's shiny pickup, which handled better than my sissy car.

I opened McNally's door. It was like opening the door to a mineshaft. The only light inside came from a flickering jukebox that hadn't swallowed a quarter in decades. My eyes adjusted to the darkness as I moved ahead, inching across the tacky floor, hoping not to trip over a body.

A barman with a thick neck crossed his tattooed arms and stared at me hard, giving his tough-guy best. It's the same in every local taproom. When an outsider comes in, the Napoleons come out. Drinkers, like dogs, are territorial.

I put a fifty on the mahogany and asked for a Coke with no ice. The barman poured it and looked at the fifty. "Got anything smaller?"

"Keep it," I said. "My friend used to work here. He said he enjoyed the camaraderie."

"Camaraderie?" he snorted, trying to stare me down. "Yeah, we're a bunch of fun-loving guys here at McNally's, a big happy family."

"My friend liked it."

"No kidding." He pocketed the bill and folded a bar towel. "Your friend got a name?"

"Vincent Dunn," I said. "Did you know him?"

His Adam's apple bobbed like Hagler's speed bag. The human beer keg put the fifty back on the bar and walked away. I sat on the stool and drank warm Coke and took in the ambience.

Bars are usually quiet during the off hours, before the after-work crowd comes in and the drinks start to flow. McNally's Tap was no exception. The few patrons in the place sat on stools with plenty of empty stools between them. No sense interrupting thoughtful drinking with mindless conversation.

The barman poured a Pabst draft for a customer at the end of the bar. He stayed down there, keeping his distance from me. I expected as much. I had violated barroom etiquette when I asked about a murdered co-worker.

An older man who looked like a regular sat on the stool to my left. He snagged the fifty from the bar. Before I could protest, he said:

"Vincent Dunn worked here for about a month. Rumor had it he was a Charlestown bank robber, one of them Irish hoods with ties to Somerville. They say Dunn was connected. He wasn't a man to screw around with."

Progress.

"You know he was murdered," I said.

"Everyone knows he was murdered. Nashua is a small town compared to Boston." He smiled at me. "I recognize your accent."

"I gave myself away."

"Up here in New Hampshire there's not a lot happening, so when something does happen, like the violent murder of an Irish hooligan, we notice."

"It's the same way in Boston."

"Dunn getting killed and dumped in the river, we're gonna be all over a story like that. It's big fuckin' news."

"It sure is," I said to keep him going.

"For the life of me I can't explain why we got so excited about stuff like that. Murders, I mean."

"A gruesome murder breaks the dreary tedium."

"It does break it," he said. "But at the same time I feel kind'a bad about Dunn, about what happened to him. I suppose it bothers me a little, him getting killed."

"Sounds like you knew him."

"I knew who he was, but only 'cause he worked here." The man shook his head. "I felt sorry for him, a big-time bank robber mopping floors for pocket change. I'd tried to show some compassion, you know, give him a buck once in a while. I know what it's like to have a fall from grace. I've been there myself."

"You're not alone on that front." I told him. "I heard the police found Dunn floating in the river in back of McNally's."

"They did, they found him in the water, stuck in the broken branches and cat o' nine tails," he said. "I was sitting on this very stool having a cold beer when the cops came hauling into the lot. Everyone showed up. The detectives, ambulances, the press, they all showed up. You wouldn't believe the blue lights. They shined through the windows and into the bar."

Too bad they weren't shining today to brighten the place. I peeled off a hundred and placed it on the bar.

"Do you know anyone who might talk to me about Vincent Dunn? Maybe someone who knew him personally?"

He swirled the suds in the nearly empty mug and carefully considered the question, but not for too long. There was money to be had, and he was going to have it.

"I think so, yeah. I might know a guy who might'a know'd him."

He eyed the bill the way a seagull eyes a clam, but made no effort to grab it. He needed more enticing. I put another hundred on top. He reached. I slammed my hand on them like a slap-jack player.

"Un-uh, information first," I said. "No more cash until you talk."

"You drive a hard bargain for a stranger." He swigged a mouthful of foam and never took his eyes off the money. "Okay, I'll play ball with you. A man named Robbie was friendly with Dunn. He comes in at three." He pointed across the room. "Robbie sits in that booth over there, the one in the far corner."

"The booth in the corner," I said. I had to take his word for it. The visibility was only ten feet. "Is Robbie a regular in McNally's?"

"Every day at three he comes in," he said. "I don't know Robbie very good. Nobody in here really knows him. Robbie keeps to himself, over there in the corner booth I was telling you about. He stays away from the crowd. For some reason or other he liked Vincent Dunn. I can't tell you why. Chemistry, I guess."

"Some people just get along." I pushed the bills toward him. Before I left I asked, "Does Robbie have a last name?"

"I'm sure he does."

"I'm sure he does, too." I smiled. "Do you know his last name?"

"He just goes by Robbie." He tucked the money into his pants pocket. "Be smart and wait 'til five. He'll be more talkative after he's had a few drinks."

"Aren't we all," I said.

5

FROM MCNALLY'S TAP I drove to an Alcoholics Anonymous meeting at Immaculate Conception Church on East Dunstable Road. The contrast to McNally's raised my spirits. The hall was bright with sunshine and cheerful with fellowship, and the smell of brewed coffee added hominess to the room. I poured a cup and found a seat in front of the podium.

After a moment of silence, the chairwoman read the preamble and asked if anyone was attending the meeting for the first time. I raised my hand and said I was Dermot from Charlestown. The group said welcome.

At the end of the meeting I stayed for coffee. A tall woman with gray hair named Dottie told me that she and her husband grew up in Charlestown. I didn't ask for her last name, and she didn't offer it. Anonymity at work.

"We moved up here twenty years ago," she said. "We wanted to get away from the city, from the hectic pace of it all, the drugs and crime and noise. And we wanted to get away from the car stereos, that blaring, obscene music."

"It's quieter up here in New Hampshire," I said, leaving out that silence drives me crazy, hence my motel room next to the freeway. "Which part of Charlestown were you from?"

"North Mead Street, next to St. Francis De Sales."

"I'm friends with the pastor."

"We lived on the corner of Bunker Hill Street," she said. "I can still smell the bus fumes pouring through the kitchen window." The memory of the diesel exhaust knocked the sentimentality from her voice. "So what brings you all the way up to Nashua, not that it's very far?"

"I'm looking into the murder of a Charlestown man named Vincent Dunn," I said. "They found him in the Nashua River with two bullets in his head."

My answer prompted a second moment of silence. The topic of Dunn's murder was a conversation ender, both at McNally's Tap and Immaculate Conception Church. To my delight, she didn't run away.

"Vincent Dunn, the jail-wise Townie." She drank some coffee. "I read about his murder, read about the armored-car heist he pulled off, too. He probably figured New Hampshire for an easy score. That's why he came up here. He was scheming to hit a bank." She tossed her cup in the trashcan. "Are you a cop?"

"I'm a private detective."

"A private detective?" She grew attentive. "Did the Dunn family hire you?"

"Dunn's friend hired me."

"Why did he hire you? I assume it was a man." Her eyes fluttered to life. "Did something shady happen to Dunn, something not on the up and up? Was it a crooked cop? A corrupt judge taking bribes? Jury tampering? Tainted evidence, perhaps a pathologist tainting the evidence?"

I should put her on retainer.

"I don't know yet, but I will," I said. "I heard Dunn was one of us. Did you see him at any meetings up here?"

"I don't think so. I saw his picture in the paper, but it looked like an old picture of him."

"You're observant," I said.

"Thank you." Her smile broadened. "I'm retired now and don't have much to keep me busy. I read the newspapers in the morning, the Nashua Telegraph, the Globe and Herald, and I go to meetings at night."

"Sounds like a good day to me."

"I'm not complaining, but I wish I had more to do," she said. "I love helping people, and not just in AA. I'd be glad to help you if you want me to. I can call my AA friends and ask them if they saw Dunn at any meetings. They might have seen him."

"I'd appreciate it." I handed her a business card, my ticket to the exit. I wanted to get out of there before she solved the case for me. "Let me know if you hear anything."

"Will do." She looked at the card. "Dermot Sparhawk. I know that name. There was a big Indian in the projects named Sparhawk. I think he was an ironworker. Yes, I remember now. He fell off a building and died. Any relation?"

"My father."

My answer led to a third moment of silence. If this kept up, we'd be as contemplative as Tibetan monks.

"I apologize," she said. "I should have known he was your father, because of the name and because of the size of you. It was tragic what happened to him. As I recall, his nickname was Chief. Am I right?"

"Chief wasn't a nickname. It was a title. He was a Micmac chief."

"Wow, a chief, that's impressive." She blushed. "I am so sorry for dragging all this up."

"No need to apologize," I said. "You didn't know he was my father, and besides, he died twenty years ago. I'm glad you remembered him."

And I *was* glad. Connections are important to me.

"You're a very understanding young man. I'll talk to my husband, too. He's a Teamster with Local 25, one of the Sullivan Square boys. Teamsters know everything." She laughed. "And they're the biggest gossips going. Those burley men with their union cards and tractor-trailer trucks, they're worse than old biddies in a sewing circle."

Maybe, but I wouldn't want to get stitched up by them.

"Thanks for your help," I said.

"I'll call you if I learn anything useful."

6

AT FIVE O'CLOCK I returned to the black hole named McNally's Tap and waited the requisite three seconds for my eyes to adjust to the darkness. After three blinks and a squint, I saw a man sitting in the corner booth drinking alone, the man I hoped to be Robbie.

A different bartender was on duty. The human beer keg with the alligator arms had been replaced by a Barbie-doll replica with shoulder-length blond hair. She was wearing a black Boston Bruins throwback jersey, number 12, with the name Cashman embossed in gold letters. My father loved Wayne Cashman. Now I know why.

I ordered a Coke with no ice, which she poured from the soda gun, and went to the corner booth to make my approach.

"Robbie?" I asked.

"Huh?" He looked up from his beer glass. "Who wants to know?"

"My name is Dermot Sparhawk," I said to him. "Can I ask you a few questions about Vincent Dunn?"

"No way, not today." He dipped his head, and his floppy brown hair fell into his sad brown eyes. "Not tomorrow, either. Vinny is dead."

"Can I at least buy you a drink?" I asked.

He stared at the table and didn't respond, which I took as a yes. I went to the bar and asked Cashman the Curvaceous what Robbie was drinking.

"Molson Canadian on draft," she said, turning to the tap. "How do you know Robbie?"

"I don't know him," I said. "I'm investigating the murder of Vincent Dunn. I heard that Robbie was friendly with him."

"He was. I'd see them talking." She poured the beer, but she seemed distracted. The head spilled over the top. "Did Robbie tell you anything about Dunn?"

"Not much," I said, keeping my cards close. "Did you know him yourself?"

"Not really." She put the mug on the bar. "Are you a cop?"

"Private," I said.

"Do you have a card? I'll call if hear something." She tilted her head and smirked. "Or if I need the services of a private dick."

I couldn't give her the card fast enough.

"My cell phone is always on," I said.

She put it in her pocket.

"Robbie might appreciate a jigger of whiskey to go with the beer."

"Pour one for him."

She poured three fingers of Seagram's 7 into a glass and put it on a cardboard coaster. I carried the drinks to the booth and placed them in front of Robbie. He muttered thanks but didn't look up. He was too busy counting the speckles in the Formica tabletop. I drank a mouthful of warm Coke and glanced at the bar. Cashman the Curvaceous was talking on her cell.

I said to Robbie, "A close friend of Vincent Dunn hired me to look into the murder."

"Is that so?"

He reached for the whiskey and took a teaser sip. I'd have gulped it in a swallow. As if reading my mind, Robbie went at it again and drained it. I went to the bar and got him another. Cashman poured it, but there was no smile this time. Had I fallen out of favor already? I brought the whiskey back to the table. Robbie gathered it in and grumbled, "Thanks."

"I'm sorry for your loss," I said. "You and Vincent were close."

"Vinny was a good guy. He might've had some trouble, but I didn't care. He was nice to me. Not many people are."

"What can you tell me about him?"

"Are you trying to trick me?" He drank beer and sipped whiskey. "Is that why you're buying me the drinks? To loosen my tongue, to get me talking?"

"I'm looking for the man who killed Dunn."

"I don't know a thing about it," he said.

People always know more than they think they know. The knowledge is hidden away in the deep folds of their minds. Open-ended questions seemed to work best.

"Did anything change recently with Vincent?" I asked. "Did he act differently? Did his routine vary in any way?"

"Yeah, I guess it did a little," he said. "I noticed a few things, nothing important."

"I'd be grateful if you told me about them. It might help me find the killer."

"I doubt it," he said. "It was nothing really."

"Tell me anyway, Robbie."

He looked at me and nodded.

"I think Vinny got involved in something that was too big for him, something that made him jumpy, like he knew they were coming to get him." He pointed to the entranceway. "Every time the door opened he jumped."

"Any idea what made him jumpy?"

"None." He moved the whiskey glass in a circle on the tabletop. "A couple of days before Vinny was murdered, a man wearing a fancy suit came in and talked to him. I don't know what they talked about, but Vinny looked worried afterwards."

"Vincent didn't tell you what it was about?"

"He didn't." Robbie finished the beer. "I didn't push him on it. I could tell he was scared shit. I didn't want to make things worse."

"What did the man look like? Height, weight, hair? Young or old?"

"Middle-aged, I'd say, possibly an undercover cop. He had that look about him, alert but shifty. He was tall and thin, but not skinny. He looked strong, like he lifted weights. His hair was blond, almost white."

"Good description," I said. "Was there anything else about him?"

"He was weird about his shoes."

"Huh?"

"After he talked to Vinny, he put his foot on a chair and buffed his shoe. Then he did the other one. He didn't just wipe them off. He buffed them with a white cloth."

"That is weird."

Robbie drank whiskey and gazed at the TV, his eyes becoming vacant. I'd better get what I needed before he blacked out. I asked him about the suit with the shoes. He looked at me as if I'd asked him the question in Latin. I tried an easier question, asking if he'd like another drink. He was too far gone to answer. I sat in the booth and pondered my next move.

The door opened and let in light from a streetlamp, causing me to look askance. A man came in, a GQ-type with white-blond hair. I nudged Robbie, but he didn't respond. GQ strutted to the bar like an important man. Cashman went to him and whispered in his ear. She handed him something, perhaps my card. He discreetly turned and stole a glimpse of me, and I discreetly pretended not to notice. Neither of us was very discreet. GQ left some money on the bar and went out the door.

I shoved my card into Robbie's jacket pocket and followed GQ outside. When I got out there he was gone. I was only ten feet behind him when he left McNally's. Where did he go? A black SUV with tinted windows stopped in front of me. The passenger window powered down. GQ was sitting in the passenger seat. He aimed a cell phone at me and snapped a picture and powered up the window. The car sped away. I didn't get the plate number.

Back at Henri's Motor Lodge I told Kid about GQ and how he took a picture and drove away. Kid told me about his day following Detective Remy Vachon.

"Did he spot you?" I asked.

"Maybe," Kid said. "Maybe not."

7

THE NEXT DAY Harraseeket Kid continued to follow Detective Vachon. I drove to the Nashua River, to the spot where Dunn's body was found in the muddy overgrowth. I was standing on the banks when my phone rang. Dottie from the AA meeting was on the other end.

"I told my husband you were investigating Vincent Dunn's murder," she said. "He knows Vincent's brother Tommy from the union. Tommy wants to talk to you."

"Is he in Nashua?"

"He still lives in Charlestown," she said. "Tommy's a Teamster, too. Local 25, just like my husband. That's how they know each other."

Dottie gave me Tommy's number.

"I hope it helps," she said.

"This will definitely help. Thanks, Dottie."

I rang Tommy Dunn and left a message. Ten minutes later he called back. After we finished with the obligatory Townie talk, I told him I was in Nashua and wanted to meet with him. He said that he was driving a load from Worcester to Portsmouth. He'd be taking 495 and asked if we could meet in Lowell. I told him Lowell was fine with me.

"Meet me outside the YMCA," he said. "I'll be there at eleven."

"See you then."

What was it with Lowell as a meeting place? At least he didn't say McDermott's Green. *That* would have spooked me.

I parked in front of the Lowell YMCA at eleven o'clock and waited for Tommy Dunn. At ten past the hour a royal-blue Peterbilt semi turned down YMCA Drive and pulled over at the curb. The airbrakes hissed. The engine gurgled and died. The driver got out wearing a quilted Local 25 vest over a checked flannel shirt. His face was neutral.

"Tommy?" I said, approaching him on the sidewalk.

"Yeah, Tommy Dunn, Vin's brother." He had a ruddy complexion, and it wasn't from the sun. He blew on his hands and said, "Thanks for meeting me here. It's on my way up."

He was a good size man in height and width, a shade over six feet and a solid two hundred pounds, a man with strong wrists and hands. When he took off his Teamsters cap, he showed a headful of dark hair clipped in a crewcut. We shook hands and stood awkwardly for a moment, talking about his brother Vincent. It was like attending an outdoor wake.

"You know Dottie's husband," I said to get things going.

"We both drive for the Local 25." He looked down the road. "What's going on with you, Sparhawk? Why are you looking into Vin's murder?"

"A man hired me to investigate it," I said. "He liked Vincent. He wants to make sure he gets justice."

"Who is he, the guy who hired you?"

"I can't give you his name," I said, hoping Tommy wouldn't push it. No such luck.

"No fuckin' way, Sparhawk. We're talking about my brother's murder. I have a right to know who hired you."

"I agree with you," I said. "You have a right to know, but I don't have the right to tell you. Protecting the client's identity is part of the job."

"This guy you're talking about, your so-called client, he doesn't trust the police to handle the murder themselves?"

Tommy had asked a fair question, one I'd been wrestling with myself, one I didn't have an answer for.

"He didn't tell me."

"What kind'a answer is that?" Tommy said.

"A lousy one, but it's the truth. All he said was he wanted me to look into the murder."

"Because he liked Vin."

"Yes, because he liked Vincent."

A block away the trucks on the Lowell Connector roared with power. Traffic is louder in the fall and winter, when the leaves have fallen and there's nothing to muffle the sound.

"I asked around Charlestown," Tommy said. "People I trust, guys with good judgment, they tell me you're okay. They say you won't stop until you get the truth."

"Your friends are too kind."

"Not really." Tommy blew on his hands again. "Do you trust the man who hired you? Do you think he's on the up-and-up?"

"Yes, I do."

He put on his cap and sort of nodded.

"That means something," he said. "If you think he's okay, that carries some weight."

A semi downshifted and made a gear-grinding groan as it came down the ramp. I waited until it stopped at the bottom.

"My client got to know Vincent at a Nashua soup kitchen," I said. "The two of them volunteered together serving lunch."

"Vin volunteered?" He scoffed. "You can't be serious."

"Vincent didn't tell you?"

"He never said." Tommy's face relaxed. "Vin serving the poor?"

We went silent amid the traffic din. A jogger bundled in gray sweats ran toward the YMCA. The hood was drawn tightly around his head. The sweatshirt seams were threadbare and the sweatpants were worn and frayed. No fancy athletic wear in Lowell.

"Tell me about your brother," I said.

"What's to tell? He grew up in Charlestown—"

"Tell me something that's pertinent to the murder. I don't care which little league team he played for at Ryan Playground."

"Very funny, Ryan Playground, playing ball at the neck," he said, and then the smile left his face. "This is strictly between us, right?"

I nodded, Tommy continued.

"Vin got in with the wrong crowd, and you know the rest of it, the armed robbery, the prison time."

"Don't forget about the man he killed in a poker game."

"That was never proved," he said. "The body was never found. On top of that, no one was reported missing. Vin didn't kill anybody."

"I meant no offense."

"I'm just saying he didn't do it. Somebody's gotta stick up for him."

"I understand," I said.

Tommy lit a Chesterfield and took a drag.

"Vin was doing federal time down there in Pennsylvania. I visited him every month, twice a month if a job took me that way." He tossed away the cig after one drag. "So I'm down there in Allenwood visiting him one weekend, and he tells me the Feds are letting him out early."

"I heard about it, good behavior."

Tommy's face clenched like a fist. It was a full minute before he spoke.

"Not for good behavior," he finally said. "Vin made a deal."

"What kind of deal?" I asked.

"I'm not proud of this." He shoved his hands into his pockets. "Vin is dead, so I guess I can tell you. God, it's awful."

"What happened?"

"He became an FBI informer."

"Holy smoke."

I should have guessed it. Vincent gets out, Vincent gets killed. It smacked of the Boston FBI. Tommy continued his lament.

"Vin agreed to turn state's evidence against his accomplices in the armored-car robbery. In return for his testimony he'd get a reduced sentence." Tommy tapped out another cigarette and tapped it back in. "A fuckin' informer. I struggled with it, my brother being a snitch. We don't do that in Charlestown. We don't talk to law-enforcement."

"I know."

"On top of that he goes and gets himself murdered, and you know what I thought? Vin got what he deserved." Tommy looked away. "I'm ashamed to say it, but that's what I thought. How's *that* for brotherly love?"

"Don't beat yourself up," I said. "We all think that way in Charlestown."

"It's no excuse."

A Lowell police car slowed down. The two cops inside looked at us. We must have passed muster, because they drove up the street.

"I want the bastard, Sparhawk." He made a fist and pumped it. "I want the bastard that shot him. Vin might have flipped, but he was my brother."

Being a Townie is complicated business. We're expected to balance family loyalty with neighborhood norms. The responsibility is burdensome at best and deadly at worst. People get killed when they violate the code.

"I'll find the killer," I said.

A tear ran down Tommy's cheek. He wiped it away and took out his keys.

"I gotta get up to Portsmouth, got a full load to deliver." He stood next to the truck. "I need to be careful what I say. I have a wife and two boys with me in Charlestown."

"There's nothing to worry about." I gave him my card. "Vincent is dead. It's over."

Tommy didn't move. I could tell he wasn't finished.

"I think Vin might'a had something to do with Tony Cedrone and Dez Barry."

"Oh, boy," I blurted.

"I know, it's bad."

Tony Cedrone from the projects in Somerville and Dez Barry from the projects in Charlestown. Two pistol-toting bad asses with multiple notches on their gun handles. If Vincent turned state's evidence against Tony and Dez, they'd kill him.

"I thought you should know." Tommy hopped into the truck and leaned out the window. "I'm worried about my family."

"I have one more question," I yelled up to him. "The armored-car heist, did Vincent pull it off with Tony and Dez?"

"Don't know, he never told me."

He revved the diesel to life.

"There's one more thing," he yelled down. "You probably know this already. The heist money was never recovered. Six hundred thousand dollars in cash vanished."

"That's a lot of money," I said.

"Dez asked me about it last week."

"Dez Barry came to see you?" No wonder Tommy was worried for his family. "What did he say?"

"He wanted to know if Vin said anything to me about the money. I told Dez he didn't, and that was the truth. Then he asked me if I knew anyone named Collings, Collings with a G. He said Collings in Monument Square. I told Dez I never heard of anyone named Collings. I think he believed me. Jesus, I hope he believed me."

"Collings with a G at the end?"

"That's what Dez said, Collings with a G." Tommy rubbed his jaw. "I knew a family named Collins, but not Collings. Now you know everything I know."

I doubted that.

"Did Dez say anything to you about Tony Cedrone?"

"What do *you* think?"

"Probably not."

"Gotta, go. I don't want to be late for the drop."

Tommy drove to the Lowell Connector for Route 495 and Portsmouth, New Hampshire. I started my car.

Two slugs in the head was Tony Cedrone's calling card, because it was nice and clean. Dez Barry, on the other hand, would rather kill you with a tire iron. He enjoyed hearing the blows mashing your skull to bone meal.

8

I DROVE TO Henri's Motor Lodge and went in. Kid was sitting on edge of the bed honing a Bowie knife on a whetstone. He wiped the blade with a rag, sheathed it in a leather sleeve, and told me about his day tailing Detective Remy Vachon.

"I followed him to a cop bar called Bressoud's Grille, a run-down joint in South Nashua." Kid leaned forward and the springs creaked. "He was talking to three guys who looked like plainclothesmen to me, and it was obvious who was in charge—Vachon. There's something about him. He's stylish and smooth, but at the same time in command. You could tell by the way the others reacted to him, Vachon was running things."

"What else?"

"They circled up at the bar and talked in low voices, almost whispering. There was plenty of tension in the air, lots of anger. When Vachon left, his crew stayed for another drink, so I stuck around. I thought I heard them say something about the FBI." Kid handed me his cell phone and said. "That's a photo of Vachon."

"You're right. He is stylish."

Somebody knocked on the door, a soft knock, not a pounding, and I wondered if it was a woman. Maybe Cashman hunted me down. I rubbed my hands together and opened it. Standing in the doorway, lighting a brown briar pipe, was Detective Remy

Vachon. He blew out the match with a stream of gray smoke and tossed it on the ground.

"Mind if I come in?" he asked, as if he needed permission.

I stepped aside and swept my arm in welcome. Vachon came in. He didn't have to worry about setting off a smoke alarm in this place. Even if there were a working detector, the wind gusting through the windows would blow the smoke away. He removed his tweed overcoat, doffed his snap-brim hat, and carefully laid them on a chair.

"You've been following me." He pointed at Kid. "How'd you like Bressoud's?"

"Nice place," Kid said.

"It's a dump." Vachon ventured to the middle of the room, taking center stage. "And you are Dermot Sparhawk. Somebody hired you to investigate the Vincent Dunn murder, somebody with quite a bit of clout."

"Why do you say that?" I asked.

"He got you a temporary New Hampshire private investigator's license, bypassing the usual protocols. That's not easy. Who got it for you, Sparhawk? Who hired you?"

"None of your business," I replied.

"I can see we're getting off on the wrong foot." He looked at the pipe. "I'll ask you again, Who's your client?"

"What part of none of your business don't you understand?"

"Christ, another tough guy." Vachon puffed until the tobacco blazed, shrugged his shoulders and said, "I was in charge of the Dunn investigation until this morning. The FBI came along and took it from me. The pricks stole my case."

I looked at Harraseeket Kid, who nodded. He thought Vachon was okay. I decided to engage with him.

"They can do that?" I asked. "They can take the case from you?"

"Technically, yes," he said. "The FBI is supposed to defer to the local authorities. That's the rule. But there are ways to sidestep the rule."

"How did they get around it?"

"They connected Vincent Dunn to a federal crime, a bogus connection in my judgment. But bogus or not, the crime gave them jurisdiction." In a voice filled with disgust, he said, "They said Dunn was smuggling cigarettes."

"There's such a thing?" I asked.

"There sure is," he said. "Smuggling cigarettes, also known as buttlegging, is a federal crime. Basically, it's tax evasion. It's more profitable than dealing illegal drugs, and the penalties are much lighter. Illicit tobacco sales are linked to organized crime, so the RICO statute comes into play."

"RICO for tobacco?"

"The smugglers buy their goods on the dark web. Or they buy cigarettes from Indian reservations, tax free." He relit the bowl. "The FBI showed that Dunn was involved with a ring of cigarette smugglers." He blew out the match. "I didn't believe them."

"Why not?"

"Dunn wasn't smart enough."

"He was smart enough to rob an armored car," I said.

"And get caught." His face remained impassive. "I fought hard to keep the Dunn case. I argued that he wasn't a cigarette smuggler, that the FBI had concocted the story. But I was outgunned. The higher-ups had a sit-down, and now the FBI has the case."

"Cigarettes," I said. "It sounds like a flimsy way to take over a murder investigation."

"That's the FBI for you." He pulled at his collar. "Nothing ticks me off more than a bunch of snot-nosed college kids with federal badges."

"The FBI has the case, and you're out," I said.

"Out on my ass."

I waited, saying nothing.

"I called a friend of mine in Boston." He set his pipe on the end table. "He said that you have absolutely no respect for authority."

"Who'd you call, my pastor?"

"You have enough guts that you can't be scared off, and enough money that you can't be bought off." Vachon then said something I didn't know, something that wasn't in the report that Captain Raymond gave me. "Dunn was tortured before he was murdered. His fingers were broken. His thumbs, too. Somebody slammed a truck door or a tailgate on them."

"How'd you know it was a truck?" I asked.

"Forensics," he said. "We got paint off a Velcro patch on the sleeve of his coat. The paint came from a white Chevy truck. It must have flecked off on impact."

"Cripes." I thought about a tailgate pulverizing flesh and bone. "That had to hurt."

"We know that Dunn was tortured before he was murdered, and we know there was time lapse between the torture and murder, but we don't know how long a time lapse."

"Any guesses?"

"Forensics took a ballpark stab at it," he said. "They said it could have been two or three hours or it could have been as long as a day. They wanted to do more testing."

"But you lost the case, and now you'll never know." I thought about the implications. "The time gap between the torture and the murder muddles everything. If Dunn was tortured and murdered hours apart, who's to say the same guy did both?"

"You're fast."

"You said Dunn was in the river a long time. Why didn't the paint wash off?"

"Luck," he said.

"The paint might've been on the Velcro before his hands were broken."

"Anything is possible."

Anything is possible? That narrows things.

"So I'm looking for a white Chevy truck that may or may not have dead skin in the door," I said.

"Or in a tailgate."

"Every third truck on the road says Chevy on it. Is there anything else you can tell me?"

"That's all I have at the moment." Vachon took his coat and hat from the chair, picked up his briar pipe from the table and placed his card on it. "It's your case now, Sparhawk, yours and the FBI's. I'd like to help you find Vincent Dunn's killer. I started the investigation, and I'd like to see it through to the end. I'll keep poking around up here. Will you keep me in the loop?"

"I can do that." I remembered something Captain Raymond told me. "I heard that Nashua has one of the best police departments around, buttoned-down."

He fitted the fedora on his head.

"Our officers wear blazers to clambakes."

9

THE CELL PHONE awoke me midmorning. I almost blew it off for another hour's sleep, but I'm supposed to be a pro, so I picked it up. The man on the other end was in midsentence. He was talking so fast I couldn't understand him. I thought his voice sounded familiar.

"Slow down," I said. "Who is this?"

"John Robinette," he said. "I saw the man with the shiny shoes."

Robbie from McNally's Tap.

"Where?"

"At a coffee shop in Concord," he said.

"What are you doing down in Concord?"

"Up in Concord," he said. "Concord, New Hampshire."

"Oh, right."

"He went into the Cleveland Federal Building. I took a picture of him and his car. It's a gray Buick parked on the corner of Pleasant and Federal. I thought it might be helpful."

"It is," I said. "I'll take care of you when I see you."

"You can take care of me by finding Vinny's killer." Robbie was a different man sober. "Nail the bastard who murdered him."

"I'll do my best."

"I'm texting you the pictures now."

Before I could say thank you, Robbie hung up. My phone pinged with the photos. I opened the first one, which showed the gray car and the license plate. The next one showed the GQ man from McNally's Tap.

Kid came out of the bathroom and asked who was on the phone.

"Robbie." I filled him in on the conversation. "I'm going up to Concord to check out shiny shoes. Want to join me?"

"As long as I don't have to drive your sissy-ass car."

The trip from Nashua to Concord was thirty minutes, and we decided to take both vehicles. Kid played games on I-93, blowing by me then slowing down, flashing the high beams and blaring the air horn. The thirty minutes passed in a flash.

I followed him down a highway ramp, and we found the gray car right where Robbie said it would be. I pulled into a space and killed the engine. Kid looped the block and parked behind me. I got out and hopped into his truck, a manly experience indeed, like mounting a stallion.

The stereo thumped with "Rocky Mountain Way," punishing my eardrums. No wonder rock 'n rollers go deaf. I watched the passing pedestrians, searching for Robbie. I didn't see him. I sent him a text message, telling him I was in Concord. He didn't reply.

"Robbie must have gone home," I said.

"Now what do we do?" Kid asked.

"We wait."

"Wait for what?" Kid asked. "What's in the Cleveland building anyway?"

"The U.S. Attorney's Office," I said.

The hours crawled by. At noontime Kid went to a deli and got a couple of sandwiches and more coffee. An hour later the man with shiny shoes walked past us and got into his gray Buick. He started the engine and did a U-turn.

"Follow him," I said to Kid. "I'll get my car."

"Got it." Kid shifted into drive. "Call me on the cell and put it on speaker."

I jumped out and Kid sped off, not quite leaving rubber. He can be subtle when he has to be. By the time I got headed in the right direction, Kid was out of sight. He called and told me he was on I-93 south. I hit the gas and caught up to him in Suncook. In Hooksett, the man with shiny shoes got off I-93 and picked up Route 3. We stayed with him through Manchester. Kid asked me how I wanted to play it, saying, "He'll notice the tail pretty soon."

With Kid's tricked-out truck, he might have noticed already.

"Keep following him," I said. "He's probably going back to Nashua. When he takes the Nashua exit, don't get off. I'll follow him from there."

But shiny shoes didn't get off in Nashua. He stayed on Route 3 into Massachusetts. At the bottom of Route 3 he took Route 128 south to the Mass Pike, and the Mass Pike east toward Boston. We drove by the Auerbach Center and the Warrior Ice Arena and Fenway Park.

"Where is he going?" Kid asked.

I was wondering the same thing. If he was going to Boston, which he seemed to be doing, why hadn't he stayed on I-93 the whole way? Maybe he picked up Kid's tail.

"Drop off him, but stay on the phone," I said. "I'll follow him from here."

Kid passed him like a jet on a runway and got off at South Station. Shiny shoes got off there, too. Kid turned toward Chinatown. Shiny turned the other way. I stayed behind him on Atlantic Avenue and followed him to the South Boston Seaport District. He parked in front of the Moakley Federal Courthouse, handed his keys to the valet, and went inside. I told Kid what was going on.

"My pal is a janitor in the courthouse," he said. "The U.S. Attorney's Office is in there."

"I know." I knew Maddy Savitz, the U.S. Attorney for the District of Massachusetts. We worked together on a case, solved it, and parted on good terms. If Shiny was meeting with Maddy, he was high up on the food chain. "I'll keep you posted, Kid."

I watched the goings-on. The courthouse flags were flying at half-staff to honor the victims of a mass shooting in Indiana, or was it in California or Nevada? I couldn't remember which. The killings ran together in my head, and I began to wonder when the next one would take place. It wasn't a question of if, but of when. I came up with a practical solution to the problem. Leave the flags at half-staff.

10

SHINY SHOES CAME out of the courthouse two hours later and jerked his head at the valet, who hustled around the corner and came back with the car. The valet handed him the keys. Shiny didn't acknowledge him in any way and then stiffed him on the tip, the miser. He got into the car and drove down Northern Avenue.

I stayed behind him.

He ramped onto the expressway and went through the O'Neill Tunnel. I followed him from three cars back. He took the Tobin Bridge and ramped off in Chelsea. I picked him up again on Everett Avenue. He pulled into FBI headquarters. I pulled over and called Kid and told him where I was parked. Kid said, "Detective Vachon was right about the FBI. I'll park at Tommy Floramo's and meet you there."

Tommy Floramo's, where the meat falls off the bone. I should have asked Kid to get me a rack of barbecued ribs.

I watched the FBI building from the car. Each person that went in was dressed in formal business attire, the men in conservative suits, the women in professional garb. No casual days for FBI agents. In the rearview mirror I saw Kid carrying two bags of food. He got in the front seat.

"I got us a couple of cheeseburger platters. The ribs would've been too messy."

"I'd have had the car detailed."

"You're welcome," he said, handing me a bag.

The cheeseburger was an excellent runner-up to the legendary ribs, and the coleslaw and fries were perfect sides. Everything tastes better when you're hungry, *and* when somebody else is buying. I sipped the last of my Coke and wiped my mouth with a napkin.

Mid-afternoon became late afternoon. A quagmire of traffic leaving Boston inched across the Tobin Bridge and emptied into the asphalt swamp called Route 1. The sky darkened. The man with the shiny shoes was still inside.

"I have to get into that building," I said. "I'm accomplishing nothing sitting here."

"You're gonna tangle with the FBI?" Kid asked. "They roughed you up pretty bad last time out."

"The art case?" I said. "That was years ago."

"What makes you think it'll be different this time? They lied to you and used you."

"But I solved the case."

"And made them look foolish in the process. Your mug probably heads their most hated poster. Think before you go rushing in."

Kid had a point.

"I'm going to Dunkin' Donuts instead." I opened the door. "You want a coffee?"

"Not coffee," he said. "Get me a large frozen chocolate indulgence with a sugarplum swirl, heavy on the whipped cream."

"I'm sorry I asked."

I walked past the FBI building. The frosted logo etched into the plate-glass window said Department of Justice, Federal Bureau of Investigation. I was looking at it when a woman came through a revolving door and called my name. She came closer and I saw her face. It was Emma Hague, the FBI agent who works in the art-theft squad, or she did when I knew her.

She had manipulated the shit out of me and played me for a dimwit, but I wasn't too sore about it. When a woman as beautiful as Emma manipulates you with flattery and sex, when she doubles over laughing at your stupid jokes, and when she pumps up your ego until it's as fat as a hot-air balloon, you tend to go along with it. I sure as hell did. She sidled up next to me and smiled as if we were old pals. She was a bitch, a beautiful and cunning and spoiled little bitch, which only added to her appeal.

"Emma," I said, feigning a smile. "It's been a long time."

"Try to contain your enthusiasm, Dermot. People might get the wrong idea."

She was still stunning, with her blond hair and flawless skin and slate-blue eyes that saw right through me. Her body movements were fluid, and the formal clothing couldn't hide it. Nothing could hide it. She was built to allure men.

"I saw you walking by the building," she said. "What are you doing in Chelsea?"

"I'm looking into a matter."

"Looking into a matter?" She smiled at me with perfect lips. "Maybe I can help you."

"Like last time?" I sounded whiny. "I'm all set, Emma."

"Come on, Dermot. It wasn't that bad. You got a big reward for the Vermeer, I got a big promotion, and the sex was greater than great." She smiled again. "I still think about you often. I miss you, you know. Did you miss me? On cold winter nights, do you think of me snuggled up to you?" She leaned forward and touched my arm. "You're a teddy bear under that hard exterior, a great big teddy bear. That's what I loved about you."

God, she was good.

"A little honesty would have been nice," I said. "We spent a lot of time together."

"We did, didn't we?" She rubbed my bicep, and my heart rate accelerated to a thousand. "We solved a humungous case, and we had fun along the way, the most fun I ever had on a case. All of life should be so good, don't you think?"

"You conned me."

"It wasn't personal, Dermot." She got in front of me. "I really liked you. I still do."

"You said that last time."

"I'm sorry for that. I really do long for you. Maybe we can start anew?"

Emma moved closer, practically becoming part of me, like Eve going for another rib. I could smell her hair she was so close. The scent drifted into my nostrils and settled in my brain in a carnal haze. She swiveled her torso and her breasts brushed my ribcage. I stepped back before I got in trouble. My thoughts alone could land me in jail. Emma crowded in.

"The matter you're looking into," she said. "Does it have anything to do with the FBI?"

"It might," I said.

"Maybe I can help," she said. "What do you say? Shall we try working together again?"

I cleared my throat, hoping to clear Emma's scent from my mixed-up head, and when I did an insight came to me. Think more like a detective and less like a jilted lover. Emma is connected to the Feds. She could be useful in this case. Use her the way she used you.

"As it turns out I can use some help, Emma."

"Is it something to do with the FBI?" She eyed me like easy prey. "Ah, it does."

"Maybe." I took out my phone and showed her the photo of Shiny. "I followed this man from New Hampshire to the Moakley Courthouse and then here to Chelsea. I believe he's investigating a murder that happened in Nashua. Do you know him?"

Emma slowly nodded her head.

"FBI agent James Graham. He works here in the Boston office. He's way up there on the chain of command. I wonder what was he doing in New Hampshire."

"How well do you know him?"

"I've never worked with him directly," she answered. "We've corresponded on cases." Her eyes met mine. "You said he's investigating a murder in Nashua. How do you know he is?"

"I said I *believe* he's investigating a murder in Nashua. I don't know for sure."

She took my arm and guided me away from the building, taking me to a shadowy alcove far from the door. Goosebumps prickled on my neck.

"Why do you think Graham is working on it?" she asked. "Who was the murder victim?"

Time to use Emma. I locked onto her eyes and told her everything I knew, leaving out that Captain Leo Raymond had hired me. She listened without interrupting and repeated everything back, making sure she had it right.

"Detective Remy Vachon told you the FBI took the Dunn investigation away from the Nashua police," she said.

"That's correct."

"An informer called you and said that he spotted FBI agent James Graham in Concord, New Hampshire. You drove to Concord and saw James Graham coming out of the U.S Attorney's Office."

"I saw him coming out of the Cleveland Federal Building," I said. "The U.S. Attorney for the District of New Hampshire is one of the agencies in the building, but there are others."

"You then followed Graham to Chelsea." She smiled, sort of. "And you are standing here, staring at FBI headquarters."

"I was getting coffee." I pointed across the street at Dunkin' Donuts. "All I wanted was a coffee and a sugarplum drink."

"And you got me instead. See Dermot, it was fate that we ran into each other. You *need* an ally like me. You need an insider who knows how the FBI works."

The last thing I need is you.

"What's in it for you, Emma? A path to the corner office?"

"Don't be like that," she said. "I just want to help. We work well together and we have fun doing it." She tugged my arm. "And we'll get to solve another case. And who knows what else we'll get to do."

Emma could be an asset if I could get past my aching heart. We agreed to meet for dinner the following evening. I walked backed to the car, feeling flustered, not sure if I got conned. I opened the car door. Kid said, "Did you get lost? Where's my frozen chocolate indulgence with the swirl? I was looking forward to it."

"I bumped into Emma Hague."

"That bitch?" He punched the dash. "That explains the look on your face."

"We're having dinner tomorrow night."

"After what she did to you?" He rubbed his face. "You are nuts, absolutely nuts. Why are you having dinner with her?"

"She's going to help us with the Dunn case."

"What?" He made a big show of waving his hands. "What the hell, Dermot."

"It will be fine. She's doing it out of the goodness of her heart."

"That bitch doesn't have a heart." If he shook his head any harder, it would have spun off his neck. "All I wanted was a frozen indulgence, but you couldn't manage it. Instead you get bushwhacked by Emma Hague. Let's get the hell out of here before you end up marrying her."

"Yeah." I started the car. "I'll take you to your truck."

"Not before I get my frozen drink." He hopped out of the car. "I'll be right back."

"Grab me a coffee while you're at it."

11

AT SEVEN O'CLOCK the next evening I drove over the Fore River Bridge on Route 3A, going from Quincy to Weymouth. The skies were clear and the moon was shining, making me feel like a Micmac Indian on a midnight raid, even though I'm only a half-breed.

I parked in the Hingham Shipyard and walked to Alma Nove, a top-end restaurant with two superstar chefs. Emma told me she wanted to meet in Hingham. I chose Alma Nove, not just for the outstanding fare, but because the owner named the restaurant for his mother, Alma, and his nine siblings, Nove. He must know Latin. Most importantly to me, he's from Dorchester, a fellow city dweller.

I went in and asked the barman for a club soda with lime. While I waited I gazed at the bottles behind him, shelves upon shelves of the best liquors on the market, imported from all over the world. I saw my reflection in the mirror amid liters of booze. The bottlenecks looked like prison bars. It was a good remember-when.

A brawny patron sitting at the bar gave me a furtive look and then looked away a little too quickly. Did I know him? He pushed away his empty lowball glass and got off the stool. He walked by me with his head down, behaving like a man who didn't want to be seen. Maybe he thought I was his mistress's husband. Maybe he saw me at meeting.

I was adjusting my tie and admiring my blazer in the bar mirror when Emma Hague walked into foyer. Any illusions of snappiness I had about myself ebbed like low tide. She made me look like a clammer trudging out of the mudflats.

She unwrapped her red shawl and handed it to me. Under it she wore a black halter dress that showed cleavage, enough to pique your interest, enough to make you want more. She was also wearing diamond earrings and a diamond tennis bracelet. Her blond hair, which was no longer bound in a bun, fell to her shoulders in soft curls. The barman saw her and overfilled my glass, splashing soda water on the floor. He handed it to me spilling more on the bar.

"Emma," I said. "You look beautiful."

The words slipped out before I could stop them.

"Thank you, Dermot. You look amazing yourself. Total GQ material. Thanks for meeting me in Hingham. I know it was a drive for you, coming from all the way Charlestown. I'll be staying at my parent's beach house tonight."

"In Hingham?"

"Yes, in Hingham," she said. "I'm staying there alone."

Not if I can help it.

She smiled at me. I gulped so hard I almost swallowed the friggin' lime.

The hostess escorted us to a table that overlooked the boardwalk. Beyond the boardwalk was a marina and a tidal river, and on the river's surface, moonbeams danced on the currents. I found the setting romantic. With Emma I'd find IHOP romantic. She opened the menu and glanced at the entrees and said, "I hope this place isn't too high-end for you."

There's the spoiled bitch I remembered.

"I'm perfectly comfortable here," I said. "How about you, Emma?"

"I dine here quite often," she said matter-of-factly. "You could say I'm a highly regarded regular, sort of a VIP. Oh, look, there's the owner. He's walking toward our table."

He waved to us and picked up the pace. Emma sat up straighter and pulled back her shoulders, ready to make a grand impression.

"Hey, Dermot," he said. "Sorry I missed you last week. I heard you stopped by for lunch."

I've known the owner, Paul, for many years. He hosted a fund-raising dinner for the food pantry I run, raising tens of thousands. He also sent his titanic food truck to the Charlestown projects to give the kids a treat. I got up and we embraced.

"Paul, this is my friend Emma Hague."

"Hello, Emma," he said, showing his winning smile. "Welcome to Alma Nove. Is this your first time?"

She was speechless, and who could blame her? Paul was fit, charming, and connected, qualities that would resonate with a climber like Emma. He is also happily married and the most genuine person I know. To her credit, she didn't attempt to flirt with him, but she managed to stammer, "It's nice to meet you, Paul." He nodded thanks.

"Dermot, I have to run. I'll call you next week on that thing we talked about."

"Sounds good."

We shook hands and he left. Emma's cheeks turned redder than her lipstick. She picked up the menu and buried her face in it until the waitress came for the drink order. She ordered white wine. I asked for a Coke with no ice. The waitress went to the bar.

"Still not drinking?" Emma asked.

"Not today."

"Good for you." She didn't sound condescending. "I'm glad. You were just getting sober when we first met."

"I remember it well."

The waitress returned with the drinks. For an appetizer Emma ordered the wood-grilled octopus. Maybe she was getting ready to wrap her tentacles around me later. I ordered oysters in case she was.

"Are you still angry at me?" she asked, not quite batting her lashes. She took my hand. "It was business, Dermot, my career. I never meant to hurt you."

"Everything's fine, Emma."

We ate the appetizers and ordered the main course. After the meal I asked for coffee. Emma ordered a pony of Grand Marnier. A friend of mine drank the stuff by the liter, until his liver pruned. Now he's dead. We talked small-talk and then broached the main topic.

"You were right about James Graham," Emma said. "He's leading the FBI investigation into Vincent Dunn's murder. They, I should say we, the FBI, seized the case from the Nashua police. Nashua isn't too pleased about it, as you can imagine. I'm not pleased about it, either."

She rubbed my hand and third-railed me. An electric shock shot up my forearm, jolting past my elbow and shoulder. My brain re-engaged after the power surge subsided.

"Are you willing to work outside the FBI, looking into the FBI?" I asked Emma, an FBI agent herself.

She said she was, and I asked her why. She told me.

"James Graham lied," she said. "He fabricated a bogus tobacco charge to get control of the Dunn case. Everybody knows the tobacco claim is bullshit, but nobody is doing anything about it. I don't like it."

Emma left out the part that she saw an opportunity to blast a hole in Graham's career and in the process advance her own. The waitress came back to the table. I asked for a refill on the coffee. Emma asked for another cognac. Her hand was still on mine, getting warmer.

"Do you think Graham is corrupt?" I asked.

She paused before answering and removed her hand.

"I don't think he's corrupt by nature," she said. "He's extremely ambitious, and blind ambition can lead to corruption. Graham has been with the Bureau for better than twenty years. He is tight with the boss, Edmund O'Dwyer."

"I know that name."

"You should know it," she said. "O'Dwyer heads up the Boston FBI office. He's one of the golden boys in the Bureau and he knows it. He has investigated the biggest federal cases in New England, all the mob stuff, and they all went to jail."

"Right, I remember."

"If you turn on the evening news, there's Edmund O'Dwyer, mugging for the cameras. He's handsome and photogenic, but he's not as handsome as you." She managed to keep a straight face. "Not even close."

Handsome? I crack mirrors.

Emma was laying it on thick, but I didn't mind. What man would? She began to talk again, businesslike this time.

"The point is O'Dwyer and Graham are tightly connected. If you take on one, you'll be taking on both."

"You're telling me to tread carefully?"

She laughed.

"Tread smartly," she said. "Don't go charging in like a linebacker."

"There goes my game plan."

The waitress placed another pony of cognac on the table and topped my cup with coffee. I added cream and sugar.

"I heard that Dunn was friendly with Tony Cedrone and Dez Barry," I said.

"I know of Tony Cedrone."

"Eight years ago Vincent Dunn was convicted for an armored-car heist. He allegedly had accomplices. Dunn did the time and kept his mouth shut."

"Do you think Cedrone and Barry were accomplices?"

"Maybe, maybe not," I said. "I have no evidence they were in on the job. I'm probably connecting dots that aren't there."

"Interesting." She finished the cognac in a single swallow, and her gray eyes glistened like rain-drenched flagstones. "I don't think I should be driving tonight, Dermot." She leaned forward and opened the cleavage wide. "Will you give me a ride?"

"I think I can manage it."

12

I WALKED EMMA to my car and opened the door for her. She was tipsy, not drunk, and I placed my hand on the small of her back to guide her in. Her butt fitted perfectly into the seat. I reached across her lap to buckle the seatbelt, and when I did, she tipped her face up to mine and parted her lips. Her eighty-proof breath warmed my throat and cheeks. I softly kissed her lips. She pulled me closer, and the soft kiss became a passionate kiss, and the passionate kiss became animalistic. The booze on her breath added to the excitement. I was tasting forbidden fruit.

We stopped to catch our breath and she whispered, "I really missed you, Dermot. I missed your kisses so much." I was still leaning over her when the seatbelt clicked.

We drove along 3A to Hingham Harbor. She held my right hand and gave me directions, telling me to drive up a hill to a side street. I pulled into a cobblestone driveway that ended at a three-car garage that could accommodate ladder trucks. The sensor lights went on and lit the property like a ballpark.

The house was a brick colonial estate with a slate roof. I counted four chimneys and three dormers. The dorm rooms were probably for staff. The only thing missing was a moat and a draw bridge. I opened the car door for Emma. She hooked her arm in mine and walked me to the house. She unlocked the wide oak door and entered a code into the security system.

We were inside.

"You call this a beach house?" I said.

"It's my parents'," she said. "They're in Florida till spring."

Good news.

Not much else was said between us. Emma led me up the stairs to a large bedroom with views of the harbor. She kicked off her shoes and embraced me.

"Dermot, take me to bed."

I picked up her lithe body and carried her across the carpeted room to a king-size bed and laid her down in it. I got undressed like a quick-change artist and lay next to her. It was a night for the record books. In the morning she was gone.

I found a note on Emma's pillow. She took an Uber to get her car at Alma Nove. She signed it, XO Emma, with a p.s. that said last night was amazing. Amazing sounded trite, something a hooker says to a john after services rendered. I've suffered worse indignities.

The p.p.s. said 'Let's meet tonight to further discuss our business proposal.' The p.p.s. reminded me of Emma's career ambitions, reminding me that I shouldn't get romantically attached. Easier said than done. The note also said that perhaps we could go to my place after we met. My place looked like a frat house after a keg party. I'd better call my friend Al MacIsaac, an ace building contractor in Boston. Maybe Al could put Humpty Dumpty back together again.

I showered and dressed and went out to my car. Tucked under the windshield wiper was a photograph of Emma wearing the red shawl she had on last night. A violent slash was drawn through her face in black marker. Written in capital letters under it was:

IF YOU CARE ABOUT EMMA HAGUE

LAY OFF VINCENT DUNN.

I called Emma and told her about the photo and the threat. She didn't seem concerned. She didn't even ask to see it.

"It's a threat, Emma."

"I've been threatened before," she said. "It goes with the job. I carry a gun and I have the FBI backing me up. I'm safe, Dermot. Don't worry about it."

"You weren't carrying a gun last night."

"You should know." She giggled. "You gave me a thorough frisking, and believe me, you didn't miss a thing. Maybe you can pat me down again tonight."

I should apply for a job with the TSA.

13

I STOOD IN the upstairs parlor of my two-family house and looked at the holes in the wall, at the smashed plaster and broken trim. I had swept up the debris months ago, but I never fixed the damage. The wall between the bedroom and parlor had been destroyed beyond repair, according to Harraseeket Kid. Thank God it wasn't a weight-bearing partition he had told me. Being a compassionate man, Kid removed what was left of the wreckage, framed the new opening and trimmed it with pine. As for the rest of the ruin, he told me I was on my own. I never got around to fixing it, but that was before Emma said she wanted to come by.

The phone rang. It was Al MacIsaac. I had left him a message on my way back from Emma's beach house in Hingham, asking him if he'd like to do repairs at my place. Al told me that he was in Charlestown today, working on a brownstone in Monument Square. Al was only a block away.

"Come on up," he said, and he gave me the address.

I walked up Lexington Street to 77 Monument Square, where Al was working. The door was ajar and I went in. The walls were torn away from the studs and the floors were ripped up. The kitchen cabinets lay shattered on the floor, and the countertops were splintered to kindling. On the ceiling I saw exposed strapping and dried cobwebs. Light fixtures dangled on their wires.

Al must be doing a full remodeling. I found him in the bombed-out pantry.

"It looks like the demolition phase is nearly done," I said.

"It's done, but I had nothing to do with it," he said. "I found the building this way when I showed up. Today is my first day on the site."

"Somebody else did the demo?"

"That's one way to put it." Al holstered his hammer like an MI5 agent and he looked the part doing it. He reminded me of Sean Connery, circa *Dr. No*. My father made me watch the old James Bond movies with him. I suppose you could call it bonding. "Vandals destroyed everything. The owners were vacationing in Europe when it happened. They came home and found this, every floor of their brownstone trashed."

"And they hired you to fix it."

"They did," he said. "I'm pricing the job now. An insurance estimator will be here later today, a guy named McClellan."

I looked down the hallway and saw a skeleton of rough-hewn studs and exposed rafters. In the front room I saw a flat-screen TV and a deluxe sound system, both covered with plaster dust. The china cabinet was filled with Waterford crystal and hand-painted porcelain figurines. The items had to be worth thousands of dollars, even on the street.

"The ransackers were looking for something specific," I said.

"Like what, two-by-fours?"

"This was no robbery."

"If you say so. I'm a builder, not a detective." Al motioned to the door. "I'm done here for now. Let's go to your place and have a look-see."

I took Al to my house on Bunker Hill Street and we went in. He looked at the rooms and nodded his head like a surgeon before a heart transplant. He was probably wondering if the same vandals came here after they destroyed the brownstone at 77 Monument Square.

"You don't have to tell me what happened if you don't want to," he said, giving me an out if I wanted to take it.

I didn't take it.

"It was a woman, Al. Her name was Cheyenne Starr. She left me."

"How come? Did you throw her through the wall?" He put his hands up. "I'm kidding."

"She got run over by a car intended for me," I said. "She lost the baby."

"Sorry, Dermot."

Why was I telling Al this? He had enough on his mind.

"She went to Arizona to rehab her injuries and never came back." I opened the closet door and took out my Boston College football helmet. "I put this on and rammed my head through the walls. I knocked down the wall between the bedroom and parlor. Harraseeket Kid cleaned it up."

Al went to the wall that wasn't there and inspected Kid's work.

"He did a nice job. I like the pine he chose to trim it out, no knots, construction grade. Excellent painting, too. I could use a man like Kid. Is he looking for work?"

"Kid's all set on the work front, but I'll pass along the message."

Al got out his tape measure and sized-up the damage. He took a pencil from behind his ear, sat at the kitchen table, and wrote numbers on a yellow pad.

"Coffee or tea?" I asked him.

He said he'd have coffee. I brewed a pot and put out a plate of Effie's Oatcakes. He bit into one and said, "Hmm, good. Reminds me of my mother's recipe."

We drank coffee and ate oatcakes, and after we finished the snack, Al said, "I could patch things up and make it look respectable."

"You don't sound too enthusiastic about it."

"I hope I'm not out of line when I say this." He moved the coffee mug to the middle of the table. "You have a great place here, good bones, but it's dog tired. It needs a complete do-over, cellar to attack, I mean attic. You need to modernize the electrical service with circuit breakers and get rid of the fuses. You need new wiring. The old knob-and-tube wires are tattered, dangerous. You definitely need replacement windows. You're heating the neighborhood. Gutters and drainpipes, a new roof, the whole bit. The granite-block foundation needs grouting and patching. I'm not trying to drum up business, Dermot. You're a good man who deserves a nice home to live in."

"I don't know about deserves." I wanted Al to feel good about the job, and I wanted him to use his talents. "Do it up. Remodel it, soup to nuts."

"It'll cost you."

"I can afford it."

He walked to one of the larger holes and ran his finger along the ragged edge.

"No plaster dust. You cratered it a while ago."

"Yeah, I did."

"Why are you fixing it now?" His face changed. "There's another Cheyenne."

"There's another woman, but she's no Cheyenne."

"Still, you want to fix up the place."

I told him I did.

"I can finish the job in a month, month and a half if I bring in my crew." He looked around. "Better make it two months. I have to warn you--the place will be upside down."

I told him I'd grab a hotel room until the job was done. I also told him about Buckley Louis, my downstairs tenant and business partner, who was confined to a wheelchair.

"I saw the handicap ramp outside," Al said. "It looks pretty solid but I'll shore it up. Tell Buckley we start early."

"So does he. I'm the slug who sleeps in." I gave him a check to get started. "I appreciate what you're doing."

He glanced at it.

"Dermot, this'll cover the whole job and then some."

"You'll have more coming when you're done." I walked with Al to door. "I'm curious, who lives at 77 Monument Square?"

He glanced at his legal pad and said, "A family named Certuse, Lou and Kathy Certuse. Why do you ask?"

"No reason."

14

I SAT BY the windows in our Navy Yard office and looked at the leaden skies that hung over the harbor. Ominous storm clouds darkened the horizon, clouds with no fluffiness, clouds that carried dread. The autumn season had been a dreary one this year, with no Indian summer and no fall foliage due to a drought. Piling on, the Farmers' Almanac called for a bad winter. One of these days I'm moving to Florida.

I slid a cup of coffee across the table to Buckley Louis. He was looking extra sharp today, dressed in a brown tweed suit, a starched white shirt, and a maroon tie with thin gold stripes. His ebony face was clean shaven, and so was his perfect head. If there is a better dressed, better groomed man in Boston, I haven't met him.

Buckley rolled his wheelchair back from the table and told me about his burgeoning law practice, which was growing so fast he started interviewing candidates for a paralegal position. I told him about Al MacIsaac and the work he'd be doing at the house.

"I'll be staying at the Hotel Abruzzi until Al's done," I said. "I'm ten minutes away."

"Don't worry about me." He engaged the brakes. "I'm staying at Shelley's tonight. Maybe I'll stay there until Al completes the job."

"Sounds like you and Shelley are hitting it off."

"It's nice having a love life again."

We both laughed. I told Buck I was going to the food pantry to do a little work, organizing the inventory.

"Call me if you need anything," I said.

I stood in the pantry unpacking cases of Prince Spaghetti, the Cadillac of pasta and a preferred delicacy of our food-pantry families. New Englanders are nothing if not sentimental. The Prince company started on Prince Street in the North End of Boston in 1912 and moved to Lowell's Spaghettiville neighborhood during the Second World War. The Spaghettiville plant closed in 1997, when Prince was sold to a food conglomerate in the Midwest.

My nostalgic musings ended when the door opened and two high-ranking thugs walked in: Tony Cedrone and Dez Barry. They weren't here for a plate of spaghetti and meatballs. Dez, a goon, grunted hello. Tony, a workout freak, flexed his traps and neck muscles.

"Sparhawk, we need to talk," Tony said, playing the spokesman.

Tony had the calculating eyes of a pawnbroker looking to fleece you of a family heirloom, whereas Dez had the wild eyes of a mick who'd happily shove a shillelagh up your ass and snap it off. I should have worn a stab vest.

"What's up?" I said.

"I'll tell you what the fuck's up." Dez growled. "What were you doing up there in Monument Square yesterday?"

"Dez," Tony said in a friendlier tone. "Where are your fuckin' manners? Set up a few of them folding chairs so we can sit and talk like gentlemen."

Dez groaned and set up three chairs and told me to sit the fuck down. It wasn't a request. The three of us sat in a semicircle. Tony leaned in.

"Like Dez was just asking you, what were you doing up in Monument Square?"

"I was talking to a builder." I answered. "He's fixing a brownstone there."

"What did the two of ya talk about?" Tony asked. "Tell me everything."

"We talked about my house." I flipped open my box cutter and rubbed my thumb across the razor, letting them know I wasn't toothless. "I need a builder to work on my house."

"Keep talkin'."

"I called him and left a message. He called me back and said he was working in Charlestown. I went up to the brownstone and met him."

Dez cracked his knuckles, getting his fists ready to throw blows. Dez was born nasty. He probably gave the delivery-room doctor the finger on his way to the bassinet. Tony, who also thrived on violence, lit a Camel cigarette. I decided not to point at the faded No Smoking sign on the wall, even as a joke. You don't fool around with guys like Tony and Dez, not if you enjoy having ten working fingers.

"Then what?" Tony asked.

"Then we walked down to my house. I showed him what I wanted done."

Dez, ever eloquent, broke radio silence.

"You were up there a long goddamn time." His red hair was thinning in front, making it easier to see the veins pulsing on his forehead. "What the fuck were you doing there?"

"I told you. I was talking to the builder. What's the problem?"

Dez sat back. Tony continued smoking and flexing. I moved the conversation forward, but carefully. I didn't want to put Vincent Dunn's brother Tommy in any danger.

"*Is* there a problem?" I asked.

"There ain't no problem," Dez said. "Quit fuckin' asking."

How many chances would I get to talk to Tony and Dez together?

"Does this have to do with Vincent Dunn's murder?" I asked.

Tony didn't say a word, but his eyes gave him away. Dez sprang off the chair and onto his feet. I'd hit a nerve. Dez, now on his tiptoes, barked, "How do you know about Vincent fuckin' Dunn?"

"Come on, Dez, everyone knows about it." I folded the box cutter and put it in my pocket. "It was in the papers, on the news, on the web. Dunn got shot in the head and dumped into the Nashua River."

"What else?" Dez said. "You know more than what was on the news."

"I heard the money from the armored-car heist was never recovered. Six hundred thousand in cash is still out there waiting to be had. Then I heard a farfetched rumor that Dunn hid the money in Monument Square."

I didn't mention the name Collings, because Dez Barry had asked Tommy Dunn about Collings.

"Why are you sticking your nose into Dunn's murder?" Dez asked. "Did some fool hire the great Dermot Sparhawk to look into it?"

"What makes you think I'm looking into it?"

"We heard things," Dez said. "Who the fuck told you about Dunn?"

"Nobody told me. Everyone knows he was murdered."

"Bullshit, somebody told you inside stuff, like about Monument Square." Dez poked me in the chest as I was sitting in the chair. I stood up and swatted his hand away. Dez got in my face. "The fuck you think you're doin'?"

"No hands," I said.

Dez remained undeterred.

"You didn't answer my question. Who the fuck hired you? Someone must'a."

"Nobody hired me." I had to give them something. "I met Dunn at an AA meeting in Nashua. The next thing I know he's tortured and dead."

"Whoa, whoa, whoa," Dez said. "Who said he was tortured? That wasn't in the paper."

"If it wasn't in the paper, how do you know about it, Dez?"

"Don't get smart with me, dick brain. Answer the fuckin' question."

I had to give them more.

"I have a friend in the Nashua Police Department. He told me about the broken fingers. Some gutless bastard slammed a truck door of Dunn's hands."

"What else did he say, the Nashua guy?" Dez asked.

"He said the Feds let Dunn out early, supposedly for good behavior."

"Whatta ya mean, supposedly?" The veins in Dez's temples pounded like stubbed toes. He'd never make it as a poker player. "Whatta ya mean by supposedly?" He repeated.

"Good behavior had nothing to do with Dunn's early release," I said. "He got out because he turned informer. He became an FBI snitch."

"No, fuckin' way Vin went snitch." Dez spit out the words. "He'd never do that, not Vin. Vin wasn't no weasel."

Tony remained silent, letting Dez do the talking. I thought they'd tag-team me.

"I'm just telling you what I heard," I said. "I heard Vincent Dunn got out early for turning informer. I'm not saying it's true. I'm saying that's what I heard."

"It ain't true. Vin's a Townie."

Tony crushed his cigarette on the floor and stood up.

"It's time to go, Dez."

"I ain't finished here."

"Thanks for your time, Sparhawk," Tony said. "If you hear any more of them so-called rumors, gimme a fuckin' call. Understand?" He took a wad of hundreds out of his pants pocket. "A cash donation for your food pantry. Stick to serving the poor. The private-eye business is too dangerous. I'd hate to see a nice guy like you get hurt."

"Me, too."

"I'm lookin' out for you 'cause I like you." Tony went on. "Some of them animals out there on the street, guys armed to the teeth with weapons, they can be mindlessly violent at times. And the thing is you never see 'em coming. They got no conscience, guys like that. They enjoy hurting people. I'm telling you this because I worry about you."

"I appreciate your concern," I said.

"That's the kind'a guy I am." He held out his hand. "Take the money."

I wondered if the bills were marked. Donating ill-gotten funds fits with Tony's value system, his version of altruism. He came closer.

"C'mon, take it. What's a matter, my money ain't good enough for you? Buy milk with it, whole milk with full fat. Those poor kids in the projects need milk for their brains. Get 'em bananas, too. Good potassium in bananas, and the fiber keeps you regular."

A mobbed-up health nut.

The money was a bribe to drop the Dunn murder, and I couldn't very well refuse it. Tony handed me the wad, and I put it in my pocket. Dez Barry stared out the window and said nothing. The quiet terrified me more than the threats. I was playing hopscotch in a mobster minefield. Tony stepped closer.

"Remember what I said, Sparhawk. If you hear anything about the brownstone up there on the hill, gimme me a call."

They exited the food pantry without another word, leaving behind a void that felt like an exorcism. I called Buckley Louis and told him about the visit from Tony and Dez. I told him about their barely concealed interest in the Monument Square brownstone.

"Check out the name Lou Certuse," I said. "See if there's any mob connections. And check out 77 Monument Square, where Certuse lives. Tony and Dez tore the place apart looking for the armored-car money."

15

THE HOTEL ABRUZZI is located on Harrison Avenue in what is today called the Ink Block. You won't find a drop of ink in the block, not since the newspapers vacated the area, but you will find high-end condominiums and apartments. The neighborhood used to be called the New York Streets, because the streets were named for towns along the Erie Canal: Seneca, Troy, Oneida, Genesee, Oswego. The streets were demolished in the name of progress, using the power of eminent domain to evict the longtime residents. The lofty ideals of urban renewal cost hundreds of families their homes, their shops, and their neighborhood--well-intended government folly.

The first case I worked on led me to the New York Streets, which led me to a clue that solved the case, which led me to riches I didn't deserve. Solving it showed me I was good at something other than football.

The only building that survived the razing was the Hotel Abruzzi, which stands in its original grandeur amid modern structures that look plastic in contrast. The hotel's proprietor is my former Boston College linebacker coach, Al Barese, the man who made me into a football player. I was standing in the Old World lobby, whose floors were finished with tessellated tiling and Oriental rugs, telling Al what I wanted to do.

"I'd like to get a suite," I said. "I plan to be here for a few weeks, maybe longer."

"I can do that." Al glanced at my eyes. "Is everything okay?"

I wondered how much to tell him.

"My house is getting renovated, top to bottom," I said. "I want to move out of there until the job is done."

"A renovation, no problem. Stay as long as you want."

"There's more, Al." I paused. "I'm working on a case."

"A case, I see."

"I'd like to use the suite as my headquarters, a place to stay, and an incident room, too."

Al, whose face is a mixture of Vince Lombardi and Rocky Marciano with a tinge of Tony Soprano, put his hand on my shoulder and moved me across the lobby to the espresso bar.

"Why don't you use your own office as an incident room?"

"The Hotel Abruzzi is safer," I said.

"You're concerned for your safety?" Al lowered his voice. "What are you afraid of?"

"I could be going up against Tony Cedrone and Dez Barry and possibly the FBI."

"You sure know how to pick a fight," he said. "Tony and Dez are ruthless animals, and everyone in the city knows it, including the police."

"I know."

"And they're still walking the streets free. What does that tell you?"

"It tells me they're protected. It tells me I should be careful. That's why I'd like to get a room here, so I can disappear for a while, go underground." I heard my own words and became embarrassed. "Maybe this isn't such a good idea. You run a family business here. A guy like Tony Cedrone will ruin it if he shows up."

Al escorted me away from the espresso bar to a corner, where no one could see us.

"To run a business like this, you have to have friends who can help you, friends who can get things done using unconventional methods."

"You lost me."

"My father once rented this entire building to members of a certain organization that needed special accommodations. The organization I'm talking about held a strategic meeting here on a Columbus Day weekend. Three days of talks. Important people attended, and we've remained friends with them."

"I have no idea what you're talking about."

"The summit I'm telling you about, it wasn't on the level of the Apalachin meeting, but I was told we had a crowd."

"Apalachin meeting?"

"Look it up. Apalachin, New York, 1957," he said. "People I know, people I trust, they've helped me when I needed help, and I want to do the same for you. I want to help you. You're staying here, Dermot."

"It's not worth the risk."

"I'm calling in the Venuti brothers from Revere. They'll hang around the lobby and make sure everything's okay. I'll assign one of them to be your bodyguard."

The Venuti brothers? That's like calling in the Marines for a playground squabble.

"Is that necessary?" I said. "No one knows I'm here."

"People are in and out of the hotel all day long. We get cabbies, chauffeurs, Uber drivers, FedEx drivers, pizza delivery people. We get dozens and dozens of guests. Someone will see you. I'm bringing in the Venuti brothers. Benny will be your personal bodyguard."

"The former heavyweight fighter?"

"The former heavyweight contender who fought for the title and lost a controversial split decision," said Al, clearly a fan. "Benny still works out. You should see him hit the heavy bag."

I smiled to myself. The potential threat from Tony and Dez didn't deter Al Barese for a second. He could have told me to find another place to stay, and I would have understood, but he didn't. He ramped up security. I think deep down he loved the action.

He waved to his brother Andy, a six-foot-seven-inch King Kong who serves as the hotel barber. Andy loves giving straight-razor shaves. The manly art he calls it. I've never had the guts to get one from him. I didn't want to become the second coming of Jake Gittes in *Chinatown*.

The chef came out of the kitchen wearing a double-breasted coat and a Chef Boyardee hat. His starched white uniform was covered with bright red dots.

"Cooking homemade tomato sauce?" I asked him.

"Andy," he said. "He forgot to strop the razor."

The chef continued his search for a cut man. Al walked me back to the espresso machine like we were doing a shuttle run.

"I have a double suite on the third floor in the rear with a nice view of Washington Street," he said. "The back suites are quieter, now that the elevated train has been dismantled. The room is spacious and private. It's my best room."

"Perfect." I told him I'd take it. "Appreciate it, Al."

"I'll book a dinner reservation for you," he said. "We have a celebrated chef visiting from Florence, Italy. If he doesn't bleed to death first, he'll be preparing Saltimbocca alla Romana for tonight's special."

"Salti what?"

"It's a traditional Roman veal dish made with imported prosciutto. Primo stuff. I still have a table for the seven o'clock seating."

"Put me in for seven."

The Saltimbocca alla Romana sounded good. I hoped the chef wouldn't need a blood transfusion before the seating.

I got settled in the suite and called Emma Hague to cancel our tentative get-together for tonight. She wasn't happy about it. I told her the date wasn't confirmed, but Emma remembered it differently. She pressured me and cajoled me and I almost gave in, but I managed to stand my ground. Emma pouted and hung up. I love it when she pouts.

I didn't want to get too close to Emma, except for the physical stuff, and I didn't want to yield too much. She was beginning to take control of the case. And besides, I was tired. A three-hour wrestling match with Emma, her version of going to the mattresses, could wait for another day. My only hesitation, she loved to get pinned.

I no sooner hung up the phone when it rang again, this time Captain Leo Raymond, the man who hired me to look into Vincent Dunn. We hadn't spoken since our initial meeting in Lowell at McDermott's Green. He said he wanted to meet with me, and he wanted it to be sooner rather than later.

"Is tonight soon enough?" I asked him.

"That's fast." He hesitated. "Tonight is fine."

"You'll have to come to Boston. I have a seven o'clock dinner reservation at the Hotel Abruzzi on Harrison Avenue. They have a veal special."

"Veal is one of my favorites," he said. "I'll see you at seven."

I hung up the phone and went to the window. A Silver Line bus sped by on Washington Street, a double-long bus with an accordion middle for cornering. It drove in the designated bus lane, making for faster travel, but not as fast as the elevated trains that preceded it. Sometimes I wonder about progress.

My phone rang again. It was Buckley Louis.

"I checked out Lou Certuse," he said. "He's super clean."

"A dead end."

"Not completely," Buckley said. "I found some archived Boston phonebooks online and sorted them by address. Ten years ago a woman named Grace Collins lived in the brownstone in question. She was listed as Collins, G. 77 Monument Square, Charlestown."

"Collins, G," I said. "That's pretty close to Collings, isn't it?"

"That's what I was thinking." He riffled his papers. "Grace Collins was clean, too. And old. She was ninety-four when she was killed."

"Killed?"

"She was taking her daily constitutional on Terminal Street when a tractor-trailer hit her. An unfortunate accident, according to the police."

"What a horrible way to die," I said.

Who the hell goes for a walk on Terminal Street? It's a haul road.

16

THE SALTIMBOCCA ALLA Romana was delicious. Captain Raymond, who was sitting across from me in the hotel's trattoria, raved about it. I salted the last corner of my meal, a charred wedge I was saving till the end. Raymond watched me bombard it white and said, "Why don't you unscrew the top and dump the rest of the salt on it?"

Our waitress came to the table, a shapely young woman from Florence, the chef's 'niece,' and she asked us if we wanted dessert. I ordered a cannoli and an Italian roast coffee to wash it down. Raymond laughed and said:

"Enjoy it while you're young, Dermot. When you get to be my age, your metabolism slows down."

Raymond ordered Maker's Mark on the rocks. I looked over at the three-stool bar. Two of the stools were occupied by the Venuti brothers. I noticed that Benny, the former heavyweight contender, occasionally eyed our table. The other brother watched the door.

After dessert, Raymond got down to business.

"How's the investigation going?"

"Lots of moving parts," I said. "I haven't fitted them together yet."

"Sounds pretty complicated." He drank a mouthful of bourbon and said ah. "Tell me about the moving parts."

I told him what I had learned so far. He listened and sometimes nodded his head. When I finished my jabber, Raymond came forward in his chair.

"So the FBI took the case away from Nashua." He gripped his glass and moved it closer to his chest. "It doesn't surprise me. Like you just said, Vincent Dunn was a federal parolee. I know Detective Remy Vachon in Nashua. He must be furious to lose the case."

"He's ticked off about it."

"The sleazy way the FBI did it," he said, "using cigarette smuggling to pry it away. What a joke that is."

"That so-called joke gave them the leverage they needed to take control."

"I don't like it."

The Maker's Mark was gone. His metabolism seemed to handle it just fine. I wondered if he'd order another one, perhaps a double this time, a double with no ice. Why risk choking on cubes when you're guzzling it down? The waitress asked if he'd like a refill and Raymond shook his head no.

"I know I told as this stuff in Lowell when we first met, but I was friends with Vincent Dunn. I offered him solid advice. Not to sound presumptuous, but I took him under my wing. Hell, I liked him." He rolled his neck and scratched his nose and might have blushed. "I already told you all this."

"It's okay."

"The way the FBI jumped in like that, taking over a meaningless case." He slapped the table. "The technicality they used to get it, I don't trust the bastards."

The party at the next table looked at us like we were louts. They were right, of course. Raymond must have noticed them.

"Sorry, Dermot, my voice gets loud when I'm upset."

The waitress refilled my cup and left the table. I raised the topic of Tony Cedrone. I told Raymond that I thought Cedrone might be mixed up in with Dunn's murder. Then I backtracked, saying that I could be making connections that aren't there.

"But I think he's involved," I said.

"Do you have proof?"

"Not yet," I admitted. "His name keeps popping up." I added cream and sugar. "That other thing I told you about, the name Collings, does it mean anything to you?"

"Not a thing," he said. "But I'm impressed you dug it up. Grace Collins, the previous owner of the ransacked brownstone."

"Probably a coincidence, Collins verses Collings." I thought of something I forgot to tell Raymond. "Cedrone questioned me about the brownstone, Tony and his understudy Dez Barry. They asked me what I was doing there."

"What did you tell them?"

"I said I was talking to the builder doing the repairs on the place, which was true. He's an old friend. I wanted to hire him to do work at my house."

"Did they buy it?"

"I don't know." I drank some coffee, shook my head, and added more sugar. "Whoever ransacked the brownstone was looking for something specific--the heist money."

"Don't mess with Tony and Dez," he said. "They're dangerous people. Even in the sticks of New Hampshire we know that much. I'd feel terrible if something happened to you."

"I have protection."

"No such thing as protection against Tony Cedrone," he said.

"You don't know the Venuti brothers."

I pointed to the café bar where the Venutis were sitting. Raymond looked at them and nodded his head in approval.

"Back to the FBI," he said. "Do you think James Graham is legitimate? And tell me more about Emma Hague."

"I'm still digging on Graham, on Edmund O'Dwyer, too. Emma is helping me with the FBI aspect of the case."

"O'Dwyer still heads the Boston FBI."

"Which means Graham will be tough to get to," I said. "The two of them are tight."

"Edmund O'Dwyer." Raymond tapped his empty glass on the table. "I remember the publicity he got when he brought down factions of the New England mob. O'Dwyer has been around for a long time."

"Like I said, lots of moving parts."

"Hmm, indeed."

The bill came, and Captain Raymond insisted on paying it, calling it a business expense. He then handed me an envelope.

"What's this?" I asked.

"A second payment."

"I haven't earned the first one yet."

"I think you have." Raymond stood. "You are doing excellent work. Take the envelope. Go on, take it."

Only fools refuse money. I said thanks. In the lobby we shook hands. On his way out, he walked by Superintendent Hanson, who was just arriving and accompanied by a knockout of a blond. They passed each other without saying a word. Strange. Raymond told me that Hanson recommended me for the job. Maybe they didn't see each other. Maybe Raymond was staring at the blond.

Hanson, never my biggest fan, reluctantly introduced me to his wife, Sharon. She was as friendly as she was beautiful, proving opposites attract. And you could tell she loved him, an act of corporal mercy that qualified her for sainthood when her time came. After the hellos, Sharon excused herself to the ladies' room.

"Your wife is a nice lady," I said. "What's she doing with you?"

He ignored me.

"I know love is blind, but it must be deaf, too."

He adjusted his purple Holy Cross tie.

"What are you doing here, Sparhawk? Do they have an opening for dishwasher?"

"I was having dinner with your pal Captain Leo Raymond. You just walked by him. I'm surprised you didn't say hello."

"I don't know anybody named Leo Raymond."

"Sure, you do. He's a New Hampshire state trooper."

"Are you deaf?" he said. "I told you I don't know him."

"You don't know Raymond?" Was Hanson toying with me? "He said you recommended me for a job."

"What are you talking about?" he said. "What job?"

"The Vincent Dunn murder."

"The Townie killed in Nashua?"

"Raymond hired me to investigate it. He said you recommended me."

"Raymond, or whoever he is, is full of shit," Hanson said. "I don't know Raymond, and if I did, I wouldn't recommend a clown like you to him. I have a reputation to uphold."

"That's what I thought."

Why did Captain Raymond lie to me? Before I had a chance to think it through, Hanson said, "How was Hingham the other night?"

"What?"

"You were seen at Alma Nove with that FBI beauty Emma Hague. I was told the two of you were having quite a time of it. What were you doing there?"

"I need your permission to go to a restaurant?"

"What did you talk about?"

"The clam chowder, and after that the weather," I said. "Who told you about it, the shifty cop at the bar?"

"None of your business who told me." Hanson looked past my shoulder. "Listen to me, Sparhawk, and listen very carefully. My wife is a sociable person, too sociable in my opinion. She'll most likely invite you to join us for a drink, probably out of sympathy because you're so pathetic. When she does, make your excuses and get lost. Understand?"

"Completely, el scram-o."

Sharon Hanson came down the carpeted hallway and joined us in the lobby, smiled and said, "Will join us for a drink, Dermot?"

"Absolutely."

* * *

Back in my hotel room I reclined on the bed and reviewed the evening's events, or tried to. My mind was stuck in neutral. I went to the window and looked at Washington Street. The brake lights and headlights and streetlamps eased the tension and nudged me toward a calmer state. I sat in a stuffed chair and relaxed my shoulders. My head slowed down and consciousness slipped away. I stayed that way for ten minutes, and in that time my thoughts unfroze and began to flow.

Captain Raymond lied to me about Superintendent Hanson, but why? He knew I'd find out about it, so he must have had a reason. I thought more about Raymond and realized I knew nothing about him. Was he really a New Hampshire state trooper? Was his name really Leo Raymond? I opened my laptop and searched Raymond's name.

Sure enough, he came up. I clicked the image tab and saw Raymond's face, the same face that sat across from me at dinner tonight. I found a picture of him receiving a medal, a picture of him standing next to a police car. I read the articles.

I called my friend Kenny Bowen. Years ago Kenny and I solved an insurance case that netted us a mammoth reward, an amount that made the money I made from the museum job look like pocket change. Insurance companies hire Kenny to recover stolen goods and to investigate potentially fraudulent claims. His company has access to almost everything.

He answered the phone. I told him I needed information on Captain Leo Raymond of the New Hampshire state police. Kenny asked a few questions about Raymond and said he'd have something for me tomorrow. Before he hung up, he said, "We have to get over to Greenberg's Nightspot. They have a top cornetist scheduled next week."

Greenberg's, the best jazz venue in the city, proprietor Ruth Greenberg.

"Sounds good to me," I said.

"Ruth will be glad to see you, Dermot."

"She runs a great club," I said. "Call me when the cornet player gets to town."

"I will do that." He paused. "Not to bring up a touchy subject, but have you heard from Cheyenne lately?"

"Not a word," I told him. "She left me for good, Kenny. She's not coming back."

The line went quiet for another moment.

"Sorry, I shouldn't have brought it up," he said. "When Ruth was asking how you were doing, I ah—"

"No sweat, Kenny. We'll get to Greenberg's soon."

17

IN THE MORNING I crawled out of bed. I should say I was exhumed from the bed. My eyelids creaked open like rusty hinges, and my fingers throbbed from excess salt. I threw on my sweats and sneakers and zigzagged to the hotel lobby on autopilot. The copper-and-brass espresso machine shimmered like a freshwater lure, hooking me in. Maybe I could flush out the salt with a jolt of caffeine. I drank a cup. It worked. I was almost awake.

The Venuti brothers were sitting at a table with a view of the entrance and elevators. They seemed more intent on playing cribbage than safeguarding me. Benny, my watchdog, slowly moved a peg. It took him three tries to get it into the hole. I hoped his trigger finger was faster. Al Barese came in and said something to the Venutis on his way to my table. He sat down and asked me if everything was up to par. I told him everything was better than par. It was a double eagle.

"Just like us," he said. "Double Eagles, two Boston College Eagles."

"That was bad," I said.

"I know."

Al excused himself and went to the front desk. I finished the espresso and headed to my room. Former heavyweight Benny Venuti watched me when I walked by. The eye contact was as close as he came to saying he had my back.

The young man at the front desk called out, "Mr. Sparhawk, you have a package." He had black hair and a fit build and a five o'clock shadow. He must be ducking Andy. His uniform, with its red waistcoat and wide lapels, made him look like a Knight of Malta. His name tag said Vito: Concierge. He handed me a thick envelope. I handed him a ten.

In the elevator my phone chirped with a text from Kenny Bowen, saying he sent a package to the hotel. I texted back that I'd received it. In my room I tore it open, dumped the contents on the bed, and was treated to an exhaustive history of Captain Leo Raymond.

I read the documents, which proved Raymond was indeed a New Hampshire state trooper. I browsed the newspaper articles, mostly puff pieces. I looked at the photos of Raymond receiving awards and citations. I saw his baptismal certificate. Leo Louis Raymond, Jr. was christened at St. Patrick Church in Lowell. I saw his diploma from Bishop Guertin High School in Nashua, his draft notice, his deployment papers to Vietnam, his honorable discharge certificate. Raymond was a stand-up guy in all areas of his life, so why did he lie to me?

I came to a stack of photographs wrapped in paper and spread them on the bed. There was a little league picture of Raymond, school photos, family photos, prom photos. I got dizzy looking at them.

One picture got my attention, a picture of Raymond wearing combat gear in Vietnam. He was standing with four men: my father, my Micmac uncle Glooscap, my late godfather Jeepster Hennessy, whose murder I solved, and Red McDermott. Raymond never said he knew my father, and he never said anything about Red when we talked at McDermott's Green.

What was going on?

I called my uncle Glooscap, my father's half-brother and Harraseeket Kid's father, and asked him if I could meet with him today. He must have heard something in my voice, because he asked what was wrong. I said I'd rather talk in person. He told me to come over.

I threw on my coat and walked to Andrew Square, where Glooscap and Kid owned an auto-body shop. The lot abutted the railroad tracks, and in the middle of the lot sat a Quonset garage. I went into the work area of the garage. Kid wasn't there.

Out back I found Glooscap sitting behind his oak desk puffing a bulldog pipe. With his pewter hair and hawk-like profile, he could have modeled for the buffalo nickel. I plunked down on the worn leather couch across from him and plopped my feet on the hassock. Glooscap placed his smoldering pipe in a chunky glass ashtray. He said it was good to see me and asked what was on my mind.

"A New Hampshire state trooper named Captain Leo Raymond hired me to investigate the murder of Vincent Dunn," I said. "Dunn was a Charlestown man. His body was found in the Nashua River."

Glooscap picked up his pipe and relit the bowl.

"Leo Raymond is one of the most courageous leathernecks I have ever had the honor to know." He punctuated the sentence with a smoke ring. "He was extremely close to your father."

I handed him the Vietnam photo and said, "Is this the Leo Raymond you're talking about, the man standing next to Jeepster Hennessy?"

Glooscap looked at it.

"That is Leo." He placed the photo on his desk and studied it more closely. "Where did you get this? Your father looks so young. We all look young. I bet it is from sixty-eight, perhaps during the Tet Offensive, the Siege of Hue. We lost two hundred men in that battle. The VC lost more." He started to hand it back and said, "Can I make me a copy of this picture?"

"You can keep it," I said.

"I shall frame it for the office." He stared at the photo as if it were a portal to his youth. His eyes blinked back to the present. "Who gave this to you?"

"My friend Kenny Bowen," I said. "I asked Kenny to get me everything he could find on Leo Raymond."

"Why do want you know about Leo?"

"He lied to me," I said. "I want to know why."

"What did he lie about?"

I told Glooscap how Raymond lied about Hanson.

"That is not very much of a lie," he said. "What if you have it backwards, Dermot? What if Superintendent Hanson was lying when he denied knowing Leo?"

"I thought of that possibility, that Hanson was playing games with me," I said. "And the truth is I wanted it to be Hanson."

"I sense a but coming," Glooscap said.

"It wasn't Raymond's only lie."

"Please explain," he said.

I didn't want to upset Glooscap. He had history with Captain Raymond. They had served together in an unpopular war, and they did it honorably and heroically. If you included my father's Purple Hearts and Bronze Stars and Silver Star, the Marines in the photo earned enough medals to fill half a checkerboard.

"Raymond never told me he knew my father," I said. "Don't you find that odd?"

"A sin of omission," he said. "Perhaps Leo did not know you were your father's son."

"Raymond knew," I said. "He followed my football career at Boston College. He knew about my knee injury. There's more. Raymond and I first met at McDermott's Green. He didn't tell me he knew Red. He didn't say anything about you or Jeepster."

Glooscap knocked the burnt tobacco from the bowl.

"This is way out of way character for Leo Raymond." He rubbed his leathery face with a big weathered hand. "I shall not rationalize Leo's lying to you, but I will say unequivocally that he must have had a very good reason."

"I need to know the reason," I said. "I don't like being deceived."

"What are you going to do?" Glooscap asked.

"I don't know yet." I looked at Glooscap's stressed-out face. "How about we have a cup of coffee first?"

18

GLOOSCAP AND I drank coffee and discussed the best way to handle Leo Raymond. Five cups later we were still discussing it. I was jittery to the point of battiness. I got frustrated and blurted out, “I hate being lied to.”

“He had a reason, Dermot.”

I couldn’t drink any more coffee, and I couldn’t think of what to do about Raymond. Glooscap said earlier that Raymond was the most courageous leatherncck he’d ever met, a hell of a compliment from a combat Marine.

“I suppose Captain Raymond can wait,” I said. “I’ll figure him out later.”

“I concur with your decision. Deal with Leo later.” Glooscap put down the pipe. “I have something you might want to see, your father’s footlocker from his days in the Marines. He kept it here in the garage, and it is still here, right where he left it. I forgot about it until just now, when you showed me the photograph. Would you like to see it?”

“I’d love to see it.”

He led me up a pulldown ladder to a mezzanine and pointed to a padlocked chest. Sitting next to the chest was a khaki duffel bag with the letters USMC stenciled in black. Glooscap handed me a key to unlock the box.

Inside I found the things you'd expect to find in a soldier's kit: a bayonet, a compass, dog tags, a P38 can opener, polished boots, a canteen. I saw nothing out of the ordinary. I picked up a sheathed knife that looked like the one Rambo carried in *First Blood*. Glooscap took it and said, "A recon saw-back Bowie knife, it came in handy in the brush."

I rummaged through the wartime memorabilia. I came to personal items: his honorable discharge pin, his 1st Marine Division patch, four Purple Hearts, two Bronze Stars, one Silver Star, and a partridge in a pear tree. I closed the lid and padlocked it. Glooscap slapped me on the back and rubbed my shoulder.

"Take it with you," he said. "You can frame the medals and hang them on the wall."

"My father never advertised his accomplishments. I intend to honor that trait. He wouldn't want billboards."

"I understand," Glooscap said.

"What's in here?" I unbuckled the duffel bag. "More military stuff?"

"Your father's work gear. He had it with him the day he fell off the scaffolding. Since his death was ruled an accident, the police gave it back to me after they investigated."

I put the bag on a table and removed the contents. I found a scuffed hardhat with union decals on it, a pair of canvas gloves worn through, a Stanley lunchbox, a thermos, a watch cap, and an assortment of gadgets and tools. I re-bagged the items and buckled the clasp.

"Is it okay if I leave the footlocker and bag here?" I asked.

"Of course," Glooscap said, patting me on the shoulder again. "You can leave it as long as you would like, and look at it anytime you want."

I left the garage and walked back to the Hotel Abruzzi, taking a different return route, staying on Dorchester Avenue to Broadway Station. A commuter train echoed under the Jim Kelly Bridge.

The cacophony faded when the train cleared the cement grotto and headed for South Station. I descended the stairs to next to the bridge and walked through a tunnel called the Underground at Ink Block, a concrete park that runs beneath I-93 and connects South Boston to the South End.

A group of local artists painted fluorescent murals on the stanchions, making colorful what would have been a gloomy underpass, creating an urban version of Carlsbad Caverns. I was admiring a fresco of Martin Luther King when my cellphone chirped with a text message from Emma Hague, asking me to call her. I did.

She said that she'd heard rumblings in the Boston FBI office, chatter she called it, and that she wanted to meet with me in a discreet location to tell me about it. I thought about her parent's exorbitant beach house in Hingham. I thought about the meal we had at Alma Nove and the sex we enjoyed afterward.

With total self-interest in mind, I suggested we go to Alma Nove, saying it was pretty far from the city, *and pretty close to the bedroom*. She said no, Alma Nove was too public a place, too easy to be seen. I learned *that* firsthand from Superintendent Hanson. Emma learned it from the threatening photograph and note. No beach house, my mood nosedived. She said she didn't want to come to my office in the Navy Yard either, for fear she'd be followed.

"What exactly did you stumble upon, Emma?"

"It has to do with Vincent Dunn's willingness to turn state's evidence," she said. "I don't want to say anything over the phone. I'll tell you when we meet."

A safe place came to me.

"We can meet in Charlestown at St. Jude Thaddeus Church. Park in the rear lot. No one will see your car back there."

"Won't the church be locked?"

"I have a key," I said.

We agreed to meet at three.

At three o'clock I unlocked the back church door and went inside. The door banged shut and echoed in the recesses, loud enough to wake up the saints. I sat in a pew near an icon of Our Lady of Guadalupe, who's a favorite of the Hispanic community. Before I got a chance to bless myself and say a Hail Mary, the door opened and Emma Hague came in, strutting down the aisle like Mary Magdalene after confession. She slid along the pew until we bumped hips, patted my thigh and said, "Is that a telescoping baton in your pocket or are you glad to see me?"

"I'm always glad to see you, Emma."

I wanted to take her into a confessional and commit sins of the flesh, but I was afraid Fr. Dominic would catch me. God would understand, Fr. Dominic wouldn't.

"It's quiet in here," Emma said. "Dark, too."

"And private, no one will see us." A soft wind blew through a cracked window in the organ loft, Catholic white noise, or maybe the Holy Spirit. "You said something about Vincent Dunn turning state's evidence. What did you find out?"

She unbuttoned her jacket and tossed it on the pew. Underneath she wore a sheer white blouse that clung to her in all the right places. The static electricity helped. If Fr. Dominic could convince Emma to join the parish, Mass attendance would skyrocket.

"What I'm about to tell you is hearsay, none of it corroborated." She turned off her cell phone. "As you know, the FBI hijacked the Dunn case from the Nashua police. The story gets nuanced, so pay attention."

"I'm on the edge of my pew."

"Do you have to joke about everything?" She shook her head and continued. "The FBI has a satellite office in Bedford, New Hampshire. When the FBI took the Dunn case from Nashua, the Bedford FBI office rightly took control of it. I say rightly, because Dunn's body was found in the Nashua River. Nashua is within the purview of the Bedford, New Hampshire office. Got it so far?"

"It's still sinking in."

"A spirit of cooperation exists between the Bedford FBI and the Nashua police. They've worked together to close some big cases. So when a Bedford FBI agent by the name of Mac Woo talked to Nashua about taking the case, Nashua went along with it, though reluctantly."

"Emphasis on reluctantly," I said. "I met with a Nashua homicide detective named Remy Vachon. He was plenty pissed about losing the case."

"I'm sure he was, but Nashua had no say in the matter. The FBI had jurisdiction."

"Because of a bogus federal charge," I said. "The FBI connected Dunn to a cigarette smuggling operation."

"Why am I not surprised that you know about the cigarette smuggling?" She kept going. "The FBI made a respectful if hollow gesture, allowing Nashua the face-saving opportunity to hand the case over to us."

"An iron fist in a velvet glove," I said. "The Nashua police gets to retain their dignity."

"Something like that."

"Where's the nuance?" I asked. "Everything you told me is straightforward."

She slid closer, practically giving me a Benedictine lap dance.

"Let's circle back to Vincent Dunn," she said. "As you know, Dunn became an FBI informer. Mac Woo was his handler. That's why Dunn moved to Nashua, to be close to Woo."

"I still don't see the nuance."

"Mac Woo met with Vincent Dunn three times in the week leading up to his murder. Woo was building a case, and Dunn was his main witness. I don't know what the case was about or who it was against."

"Then how do you know he was building one?"

"An educated guess," she said. "The things I'm telling you are uncorroborated."

"Uncorroborated?" It sounded like bullshit. "Keep going."

"I'll probably never know what Mac was up to. He doesn't trust the Boston FBI office, and he refuses to talk to me about it."

Something screwy was going on here, something Emma wasn't saying. Why didn't Woo tell Emma about the case? I looked at Emma's hungry eyes and eager face and ready posture. Ambition was written all over her. I bet Woo didn't trust her, knowing she's a climber.

"Why would Mac Woo open an investigation with a convicted bank robber as the main witness?" I asked.

"I don't have an answer."

"Using a felon to testify? To build a case? Who'd believe him?" I looked at tabernacle and the perpetual burning candle. "That's stooping to a pretty low threshold, even for the FBI."

She ignored my jab and continued.

"All I can tell you is Mac was building a case using Vincent Dunn in New Hampshire, and then along comes the Boston FBI, who governs the New England region. They removed Woo as Dunn's handler and replaced him with James Graham."

"Graham, O'Dwyer's handpicked man," I said.

"James Graham is in. Mac Woo is out. Not only is Mac out, but he's been quashed. He can't say a thing about Vincent Dunn or the case they were working on. If Mac utters a word about it, Edmund O'Dwyer will send him to an outpost in Alaska."

"I thought the Catholic Church was tough."

"And no one would miss him, either," she said. "We have six hundred field agents in the New England region. People get transferred all the time."

"Woo got screwed."

"Welcome to the FBI."

I put my arm around Emma's shoulder and listened to the wind whooshing through the cracked window, a breathing sound that made me feel like a baby in a mother's womb. Our Lady of Guadalupe, pregnant with child, looked down at me. Emma nuzzled closer and then then pulled away. A church pew isn't the most romantic setting. She asked me if I knew a Charlestown man named Eddie Loan. I told her I did and asked her why.

"His name came up in our inquiries."

"Inquiries to do with Dunn's murder?" I asked.

"Not the murder, the armored-car heist from eight years ago," she said. "We never found the money. We never caught Dunn's accomplices, either. We know he didn't do it alone."

"And you think Eddie Loan was an accomplice?"

"All I'm saying is his name came up." She sat upright in the pew and looked at her watch. "I'm just telling you what I heard."

I thought about Eddie Loan as a bank robber.

"No way Eddie was involved with Dunn. He donates to the food pantry."

So did Tony Cedrone.

"I'm just telling you what I heard," she said again.

"I'll talk to him, Emma."

"Good, and don't underestimate the importance of Mac Woo. Something happened in New Hampshire. I believe Mac can fill you in *if* you can get him to talk."

"I'll look into Mac Woo, too," I said.

Then a sad thing happened. Emma put on her jacket, covering her clingy shirt and all it clung to. The wind stopped howling in the loft. The eternal flame flickered and nearly went out. I stopped fantasizing about Emma in a crammed confessional. She got up and left the church.

Our Lady of Guadalupe looked relieved.

19

I WALKED TO my office in the Charlestown Navy Yard. Buckley Louis was dressed mannequin sharp, wearing a cadet-gray suit and a navy-blue tie with a perfect Windsor knot that featured the telltale dimple. Harraseeket Kid was there too, and he too was looking sharp, wearing stonewashed denim from head to toe, cowboy boots, and a ponytail held in place with a copper clip. I told them about the meeting with Emma Hague and asked them what they thought about it. Kid started it off.

"Emma told you Mac Woo was important." He rubbed his bronze cheeks with both hands. "Call your man Kenny Bowen. Ask him to do a background check on Woo. Ask him to look into the FBI office in Bedford, New Hampshire. You need to know who you're dealing with up there. Kenny can dig up that kind'a stuff."

"I agree Woo was part the case," I said. "But he basically served as a way station until the Boston FBI took over. How much can he know?"

"Woo was more than a way station," Buckley said, siding with Kid. "Woo was building a case, and then he was completely humiliated, stomped on by Boston."

"You're saying Woo might be ticked off that O'Dwyer and Graham stole the case from him," I said. "I didn't think of that."

"If he *is* ticked off," Buckley added, "he might give us something we can use."

"Woo's gotta be pissed as hell," Kid said. "Vachon, too. The Boston FBI duped them, treated them like amateurs."

"I'll call Kenny."

Buckley rolled across the room to the windows that faced Dry Dock 2. I got up and stood next to him. The skies had turned dark and the streetlights flickered to life, dull at first and then brightening. Buckley popped a mini wheelie and said, "What about the other name Emma Hague mentioned, Eddie Loan?"

"Emma implied that Eddie was in on the armored-car heist with Dunn," I said. "Dunn's accomplices were never caught."

"Townies." Kid laughed. "They don't say nothin' to no one."

"If Dunn had an accomplice, it wasn't Eddie Loan," I said. "He's not that kind of guy." I thought about the volunteer hours he put in at the food pantry, the compassion he had for the poor. "Eddie's name came up for a reason. I'll give him a call."

"It's good to be thorough," Kid said. "Eddie might be innocent, but he might know things we don't know. It's good you're talking to him."

The moon was low and climbing. Buckley rolled back to his desk. Kid plugged in the coffeemaker and started a pot. I stayed at the window. It was time to get cracking.

"I'll call Kenny Bowen about Mac Woo, and I'll talk to Eddie Loan."

"I'll look into the Boston FBI, paying close attention to the honcho, Edmund O'Dwyer," Buckley said.

"Don't forget about James Graham, O'Dwyer's protégé." I added.

"I'll follow James Graham." Kid poured half a cup while the machine was still brewing and topped it with cream. "I don't like him. He's a bully with a badge."

We had our assignments.

I went to my room in the Hotel Abruzzi and ordered supper from the trattoria. Twenty minutes later the meal arrived, a slab of lasagna the size of a red brick with plenty of sauce. I grabbed a knife and fork, and the sparks flew. I finished the colossus and called Kenny Bowen.

I told him what I needed. He said he'd research Mac Woo and look into the Bedford, New Hampshire FBI office. We agreed to meet at eight o'clock the next evening at Greenberg's Nightspot. I thanked him and hung up.

Next task, Eddie Loan.

I called Eddie and asked him if we could get together to discuss Vincent Dunn, telling him I was looking onto the murder. Eddie said he had time tomorrow and asked if lunch was okay? I said lunch was fine.

"I'll be photographing the Waterworks Museum across from the Chestnut Hill Reservoir," he said. "The City of Boston designated it a landmark."

"You don't say."

"Which obviously you don't care about. How about Pino's at noon?"

"I'll see you at Pino's," I said.

I clicked off the lights and fell asleep with a bellyful of lasagna, wondering if it noodles were made by Prince.

20

EACH TIME I drive by Chestnut Hill and Boston College, I think back to the Jesuits who taught me and the coaches who molded me. And each time I drive by Alumni Stadium my knee aches psychosomatically, and I know it's psychosomatic because sometimes the good knee aches.

The best cure for the Chestnut Hill blues is a hot meal at Pino's Pizza. I drove down Beacon Street, dodged a Green Line trolley, and parked in Cleveland Circle. At the pizzeria counter I told the old paisano I'd have a large pepperoni, sausage, and onion pizza with extra oil. No sense skimping. I had called Eddie Loan before ordering, and he was onboard with the cholesterol pie. Twenty minutes later a bubbling jumbo came out of the oven at the same time Eddie came through the door. Perfect timing.

We grabbed a booth, ate, and talked about Boston sports. After one slice Eddie pushed his paper plate aside, leaving me the chore of eating the rest.

"On the phone you mentioned my friend Vincent Dunn," Eddie said. He spoke with such reverence I thought he was talking about the pope, not a convicted criminal. "Vin and I were close as kids. We ended up going our separate ways, but we were close at one time. I saw his brother Tommy at the wake and funeral. He took it hard."

"I know Tommy," I said.

Eddie was in his mid-fifties with nary a thread of gray in his full head of brown hair. I asked him why he stopped hanging around with Vincent. Townies usually stayed friends for life. Eddie looked over his shoulder and lowered his voice.

"Vin is dead, so I guess I can talk about it. He got into some things I didn't agree with. But I figured that was his business, so I overlooked it at first. Then came rumors of the poker game. I stopped calling him after that."

"I heard he beat a man to death at the game," I said. "Do you think it's true?"

Eddie slid out of the booth.

"You want coffee?"

"A large regular," I said.

He went to the counter and returned with two cups, giving me the large. One of these days I'm going to percolate. Eddie's brow furrowed. I asked him if he was okay.

"I'm fine," he said. "Why are you asking me about Vin? I don't know anything about his murder."

Eddie's name had come up as a person of interest in the armored-car heist, but I couldn't tell him that. He'd freak. Any law-abiding person would. I played with my cup and said, "Maybe Vincent was murdered because of the poker game."

"Do you think the two are connected, the poker game and Vin's murder?"

"I think it's possible," I said. "What do you think?"

"I don't think so." Eddie answered. "The alleged poker game was twenty years ago. Who waits twenty years to kill someone?"

"Vincent is dead."

"Twenty years after the game," he said.

I tore off another slice.

"What if the poker game was nothing but a hoax?" I speculated. "What if it never happened? The police never found a body."

Eddie twirled the pizza tin like a roulette wheel.

"It happened," Eddie said and looked around. "I was there."

"You were there?" I said too eagerly. "You saw it?"

Eddie rapped his knuckles on the table and looked at me.

"Between us?"

"Yes, Eddie, between us."

He shifted his body into the corner of the booth.

"I used to enjoy playing poker with the guys in Charlestown. The games had an edge to them, man against man, not man against the house. I've been to Atlantic City, Las Vegas, Reno, with their theme parks and amusement rides and all-night buffets. There's no tension in the air. In Charlestown, the stakes were more than the money in the pot."

"Tell me about the game."

He spun the pie plate again.

"The game was going along as usual. Drinking and smoking, everybody having a good time. A new guy was at the table, an out-of-towner with money, cocky as hell. He was wearing a flowery Hawaiian shirt and bright yellow pants and sandals. He was a flake, or pretending to be. It was hard to tell. He could have been playing us."

"What happened?"

"The game got tense late in the night, big pots, money flying around. One of the pots piled up. Vin kept raising. The flake kept seeing his raise and re-raising him, and then he called Vin. Vin wasn't bluffing. He had three aces. But the flake beat him with a straight."

"That had to sting."

"Winning wasn't enough for this guy. He taunted Vin and started singing 'You gotta know when to hold 'em, know when to fold 'em.' Then he broke into 'If I only had a brain.' Vin reached across the table and gave him backhander. The flake grabbed a hammer from a tool bag on the floor—one of the players was a builder--and went at Vin. Big mistake. Vin wrestled the hammer away from the guy and whacked him on the noggin. Blood sprayed everywhere."

"Jesus."

Eddie winced at the memory of it.

"The thing is Vin didn't have to do it," he said. "He took the hammer from the flake, got it away clean. It should have ended there, but it didn't."

"Vincent let him have it," I said.

"I never spoke to Vin again," he said. "I never played poker again, either."

"If I saw something like that, the closest I get to a deck of cards would be solitaire in a locked room." I thought about what Eddie told me. "Vincent got away with it."

"I kept expecting to see the flake's face on the news," Eddie said. "Weeks passed and nothing happened. A month went by, still nothing. No one was reported missing. I started wondering what might have happened, making up scenarios in my head. Maybe the flake was passing through town on his way to someplace else. Maybe he stopped in Boston for a night and nobody knew he was here."

"Maybe the flake survived the attack and walked away." I suggested. "Or maybe somebody took him to the hospital."

"No way in hell, Dermot. The hammer was one of those framing hammer with a long handle. The claw tore into the flake's scalp like a pickax. He was dead."

"Bang, bang, Maxwell's silver hammer came down upon his head," I said. He didn't think it was funny. "Sorry, Eddie."

"I couldn't call the police," he said. "I had kids to think about, a home to protect. Rats don't last long in Charlestown, not in those days, not in the real Charlestown."

"My father told me what it was like back then." I didn't have the heart to tell Eddie that Vincent became an FBI informer. I switched topics. "Does the name Grace Collins mean anything to you? She lived in a brownstone at 77 Monument Square."

Eddie said he didn't know anyone named Grace Collins. I told him about my run-in with Dez Barry and Tony Cedrone at the food pantry, and how they quizzed me about 77 Monument Square.

"What did you tell them?" Eddie asked.

"I told them the truth. I said I was meeting a contractor there named Al MacIsaac. Al was rebuilding the brownstone that somebody ransacked. I told them I wanted to hire Al to work on my house." I then talked about the heist that landed Dunn in prison. "The money was never recovered. Six hundred thousand dollars in cash is still out there. I think Tony and Dez were looking for it in the brownstone."

"Tony and Dez thought it was in the brownstone?" I could tell Eddie didn't buy it. "That money is long gone. No one sits on six hundred grand for eight years."

"Unless he's in prison," I said.

Eddie stirred on the bench and slid to the center. He was directly in front of me.

"The FBI questioned me about the heist when it happened." He picked up the napkin dispenser and put it down. "They said my credit card was used to pay for a hotel room that Vin might have stayed in after the job."

"Vincent stole your credit card?"

"Not Vin," hc said. "A cocktail waitress he knew stole it. I'm pretty sure it was her. She worked at the Tally Ho Lounge near the Garden. I'd go there before Bruins games. I found out later that she was a connected to the Somerville mob."

"Why did she steal your card?" I asked. "Why not a stranger's?"

"I thought the same thing, why me? I think I figured it out. Vin told her to. He knew I was smart enough to play dumb if the cops asked me about the card, which they did."

"And you didn't say anything?"

"Of course not," he said. "Vin guessed right. I was smart enough to play dumb. Plus, I didn't want Somerville breathing down my neck. I told the FBI I knew nothing about the card or the hotel. They never questioned me again."

"They dropped it?"

"Yeah, they did, and I think I know why. I reported the card missing a day or two after I noticed it was gone. That must have worked in my favor."

A young Hispanic woman came out to clear the tables. She carried the loaded bus bucket back into the kitchen. When the swinging door closed behind her, Eddie began to talk again.

"Vin and I did everything together as kids. Altar boys, little league, Pop Warner football, hockey, swimming in the Doherty pool. We used to reenact the Battle of Bunker Hill on the Seventeenth of June, Bunker Hill Day. We pretended to be the colonials, armed with broken hockey sticks as muskets, defending our turf against the Red Coats."

"Sounds like innocent fun."

"We parted on good terms I think. He understood I didn't want to be a criminal, and he never tried to get me to join him. Vin had a good heart." He reached for his jacket and slid out of the booth. "The poker game we talked about—"

"It's between us," I said.

We shook hands and Eddie left Pino's.

I sat and wondered about the six hundred thousand. Maybe Vincent Dunn was killed for the heist money and not for turning informer.

I had to figure this thing out before more people got hurt, or worse, killed.

21

FROM CLEVELAND CIRCLE I drove to the Hotel Abruzzi, changed into my sweats, and drove to the L Street Bathhouse for a workout. After a brisk warmup, I pedaled the Schwinn Airdyne for twenty minutes, doing my best to work off last night's lasagna and today's pizza. I got good and sweaty and hit the weight room. After the weights, I stretched on the mats, focusing on the lower back and hamstrings, and from the mats I jogged to the car.

Back at the hotel I took the longest, hottest shower in the history of indoor plumbing. I toweled off like a Roman emperor, put on a Turkish bathrobe, and studied the incident board. The names and locations and times were connected by dotted lines and arrows. The chart showed no solid lines, no definitive conclusions. It didn't clarify a thing. If anything, the crisscrossing scribble confused me. Data analysis was never my strength.

I relaxed on the bed atop the covers. In two hours I'd be meeting Kenny Bowen at Greenberg's Nightspot to discuss Mac Woo, the New Hampshire FBI agent who took the Dunn case from the Nashua police. Once he got it, the Boston FBI took it from him.

I dressed in wool pants, a blue jacket, a white shirt, and a tattered red tie that had seen better days. The whole getup had seen better days. I thought about ditching the tie, but I remembered something Kenny said to me. Ruth Greenberg, the club's ravishing owner, was asking about me. I kept the tie on.

In the lobby on my way to the car, the hotel tailor, Don DeRosa, waved me into his shop. A distinguished-looking man from Milan, Italy, Don works with the finest fabrics in the world, and he travels throughout Asia and Europe to buy them. Al Barese once told me that Don is a maestro on the sewing machine, the Liberace of Singer.

I went in to Don's inner sanctum.

Around his neck he wore a tape measure, and in his hand he held a flat piece of chalk. Don doesn't speak English, but he is fluent in fashion. He looked at me and said, "No, no, no."

"What do you mean?" I asked.

Don removed the oil rag I called a tie and threw it in the trash. He handed me a gold one with purple swirls. I never saw such a beautiful tie. He gestured for me to put it on. I knotted it and nodded my thanks. Don shook his head and signaled for Al Barese to join us. They spoke in Italian. Al told me to give him the tie.

"You tied it with a Windsor knot," Al said. "Don recommends a four-in-hand knot."

"A what?"

"The four-in-hand results in a longer, more vertical knot, like an isosceles triangle, which better suits your longish face. The Windsor renders a blockier knot for a man with a square face."

"You have to be kidding."

"Do you see Don laughing?" Al asked.

Don demonstrated the correct way to form a four-in-hand knot. I should have taken notes. I put it on, snugged it to my throat, and started for the door.

"Wazza madda you?" Don said. He took my sports coat and pressed it on a professional ironing board, shook his head, and threw it in the trash. He went to the coatrack and picked out a blazer. He said something to Al, who translated. "Midnight blue, made of virgin cashmere from India." Don asked for my shirt and steam pressed it, sized it up, and added it to the trashcan. "Terrible, bad."

"I just washed it," I said, getting defensive.

"Is okay, is okay," Don assured me, patting my arm.

He unboxed a shirt, ironed it, and handed it to me. Al, interpreting, said, "Egyptian broadcloth, French blue, a perfect match for the gold tie and midnight blue jacket."

"I feel like yankee doodle dandy."

Don wanted my pants next. I took them off and threw them in the trash, saving him the trouble. He measured me.

"Lungo," he said. "Molto lungo."

"That means very long," Al told me.

Sadly, he was measuring the inseam, not the crotch. Don tailored the pants. Al again, "Wool gaberdine trousers from England, charcoal gray."

I was down to my briefs, like a boxer at weigh-in. Don pointed at my sagging socks, which didn't match. Off with the old socks, on with the new ones, which were black with dark blue clocks. I put on my new clothes and said, "Grazie."

"Prego." Don looked me over. "Fantastico! Go see belladonna."

I came in looking like Columbo and went out looking like James Bond, going from zero to 007 in seconds.

"I'll add the socks, shirt, coat, pants, and tie to your bill," Al said with a smirk.

"I'm glad he doesn't sell luxury cars."

"Don wants to see you tomorrow. He said you need a proper suit."

"A proper suit?" I said. "I never wear suits."

"He's making you one."

"I'll save it for my funeral. It'll give me incentive to stay in shape."

"We all need a reason to stay in shape," Al said.

Things were looking up. The last time I got fitted for a suit it was for a straitjacket in a dry-out joint. I grabbed one of Don's business cards and left the hotel to meet Kenny.

I found parking on Columbus Avenue, a block away from Greenberg's Nightspot. Inside I saw Kenny Bowen sitting at a table near the stage. Jazz pianist Zack Sanders was playing a familiar number, but I couldn't tell you the name of it. Zack was dressed in his customary black tux, black satin bowtie, black patent-leather loafers, and black onyx cufflinks, all of which matched the black lacquered Steinway grand, which complemented his rich ebony skin. He nodded when I went by and said, "Lookin' sharp, Dermot."

I thanked Kenny for meeting me and sat at the table with him. Kenny is a former Olympic shot putter. He also competed for Dartmouth College, where he set Ivy League records in the shot and discus. His shorn head and Native American features added to his formidable presence. Like me, Kenny is half Indian. Unlike me, he doesn't have a yen for the hooch.

"Nice suit," he said. "I get my stuff custom-made, but nothing that posh."

"I got ambushed by a tailor." I handed him Don DeRosa's card. "The Hotel Abruzzi in the Ink Block, that's where you'll find him."

"Believe me, I'll find him."

He stirred his scotch on the rocks and asked me how the Dunn case was progressing. I told him baby steps, and then I corrected myself and said infantile crawling. Kenny laughed and placed a notepad on the table and opened it to the first page.

"FBI agent Mac Woo is the definition of an eclectic man. He grew up here in Quincy, in the Montclair section, finished first in his class at North Quincy High School, and accepted a full academic scholarship to Cornell."

"Smart guy."

"Extremely smart. Woo double majored in accounting and English at Cornell. He was again class valedictorian. He then went to NYU Law to be near the Greenwich Village literary scene. He loved the Beats, particularly Kerouac and Ginsberg and Henke. Woo dove headlong into the Village poetry community, reciting his work at coffeehouses. At the same time he was editor of the law review at NYU. Any smarter and he could have gone to Dartmouth."

"He'd have broken your shot put record." I thought about Woo's bio. "A poet-bohemian in the FBI? It sounds like a mismatch."

"Mismatch is an apt word for Woo. The name Mac is short for MacArthur. His parents were Chinese immigrants and they named him after General Douglas MacArthur."

"That shoots down my half Scottish-half Chinese theory."

Zack Sanders hit the piano keys and said, "Woody Herman's *Woodchopper's Ball*, from the Big Band era."

Ruth Greenberg came to the table and said hello to us. Her long black hair tumbled to her shoulders in loose curls. Her white dress shirt and black slacks were fitted to her body, perfectly fitted I'd say.

"Coffee, Dermot?"

I said yes to the coffee and managed not to drool. Ruth leaned closer and said she adored my gold and purple tie, and then she rubbed the cashmere blazer. I should get dressed up more often. She turned and went to the bar, her hips swinging with each step. I liked Ruth. She walked like she meant it.

"I told you she was keen on you," Kenny said.

"She was keen on my tie," I said. "I've ruined enough women's lives."

"Ruth can handle herself." He drank some scotch. "She's more than capable of handling a man of your caliber, first-class guy that you are. Ask her out."

"Back to Mac Woo."

Kenny smiled.

"He finished law school, got married, realized he wasn't the second coming of Charles Bukowski, and looked for a paying job. He got one with the FBI and did extremely well. The Bureau had plans for Woo. They assigned him to the Boston office, where he quickly became a rising star. Then something happened. Nobody could tell me what it was, but Woo's fast-track career was derailed. The Boston FBI transferred him to Bedford, New Hampshire, the hinterlands of the New England FBI."

Ruth returned with a carafe of coffee, a mug, and a plate of creamers and sugar packets. We smiled at each other, and I damn near choked on my Adam's apple. Yesterday it was Emma Hague, tonight it was Ruth Greenberg. Could life get any better?

On stage Zack said, "For Dermot Sparhawk," and played *Ain't that a Kick in the Head*. I quietly sang along, pretending I was Dean Martin, my mother's heartthrob. When the song ended, Kenny and I picked up the conversation.

"So Woo got booted from Boston," I said. "Did Edmund O'Dwyer and James Graham get rid of him?"

"It's very possible." Kenny splayed his banana fingers on the table. "I couldn't get much info on O'Dwyer and Graham. The Boston FBI office is a territorial fortress, and in my opinion, prone to corruption. I have no evidence to support my claim, but I've heard things from people I trust."

I poured coffee.

"You think they're corrupt?"

"I have no proof." Kenny finished his scotch. The waitress asked him if he'd like another one. He said no and asked for a coffee mug. "As you know, I have dealings with many organizations across the country, around the world, actually. They all cooperate to some degree, some more than others. Every law-enforcement agency is guarded, but usually I can get something out of them. I couldn't get squat out of the Boston FBI. And that's after a senator made a call on my behalf."

"You went to the top."

"You'll get my bill." The waitress delivered the mug. Kenny poured a cup from the carafe and drank it black. "The point is I didn't get jack on Boston."

"Maybe you can discount the bill."

We swigged coffee and listened to the piano.

"Fats Waller," Zack said, "*Ain't Misbehavin'* and then *Moon River* by Henry Mancini."

The evening went along at a syncopated pace, and two hours later it came to a rhythmic end. Kenny and I applauded Zack Sanders and loaded up his tip jar. We then went to the bar and said goodbye to Ruth Greenberg. Outside on Columbus Avenue the frosty air shivered the neighborhood, keeping South Enders inside. It was so quiet you could hear the streetlights humming above. Kenny buttoned his overcoat to the top.

"Will you talk to Mac Woo?"

"I'm planning to," I said. "It will give me something to do. I'm not exactly inundated with leads."

"It could be a dead end."

"Most leads are dead ends." I turned up my collar. "Any suggestions on how to best handle him?"

"Talk to Woo in person, not on the phone," Kenny said. "Approach him directly. Don't go through the Boston FBI. They dumped him, and they might be looking for ammo to use against him. Woo is tight with the Nashua police. They respect him. Maybe you can get something going up there."

I thought about Nashua police detective Remy Vachon.

"I'll talk to Woo."

"Gotta run," Kenny said, adding, "I miss seeing you at the gym."

"I'll get there soon."

"It's important to stay fit, Dermot."

"Everyone keeps telling me."

Kenny manages an austere gym under the stands of Harvard Stadium, where former Ivy League athletes train. I'm the token proletariat.

"I worked out at the L Street Bathhouse today," I said in my defense.

"I knew you worked out. The veins in your wrists and hands were throbbing tonight."

"That was from Ruth Greenberg."

"Go home and get some sleep, Dermot."

22

I MET BUCKLEY Louis and Harraseeket Kid the next day in our office. The always stylish Buckley was wearing a two-button Armani suit with a tonal stripe. The ever-rugged Kid was dressed in Wrangler jeans and engineer boots. I told them what Kenny Bowen told me about Mac Woo, and about Woo's strong rapport with the Nashua police.

Kid told us about his day tailing James Graham, saying that he followed him to the FBI office in Bedford, New Hampshire, where Graham stayed for two hours. Graham then went to his Wellesley home, a sprawling Tudor house with an in-ground pool and a tennis court, pretty good digs for an FBI agent.

"I forgot to mention the two-car garage and two Mercedes," Kid said. "The peckerhead has to be crooked."

Buckley told us about the research he'd done on Edmund O'Dwyer, head of the Boston FBI office. On the surface O'Dwyer looked like a 21st-century Elliot Ness.

"Something doesn't add up with O'Dwyer," Buckley said. "Something stinks."

"Like what?" I asked.

"Like the way he handled Mac Woo." He wheeled back. "By all accounts, Woo was an outstanding agent, doing an outstanding job, and then bang, he's out—reassigned to backcountry New Hampshire. No explanation was given. And then there's

O'Dwyer's finances, which don't make sense. His assets are way out of whack with his reported income. He owns a manor in pricy Weston on a three-acre lot off Boston Post Road. He has an oceanfront home in Key West for when it gets cold, and a Boston Whaler cabin-cruiser for when it gets hot. Expensive cars, too."

"You're right, it stinks," I said.

"I'll keep digging. What's next for you, Dermot?"

"I'm going to New Hampshire to talk to Mac Woo."

We agreed to meet later for an update.

I ramped onto I-93 north and put the hammer to the floor. Everyone else in the state drives like a maniac. I might as well join them. An hour later I parked in the FBI lot in Bedford, getting there lickety-split. For some reason I thought about the compactness of New England. You could fit the six state region into Montana twice with room left for Delaware.

I went into the lobby and that's as far as I got. The receptionist, a feisty woman with granite hair, stonewalled me at the desk, saying that Mac Woo was not available. I told her it was important that I talk to him. She didn't care what I thought was important. I left my name and number, hoping she wouldn't tear it up, and walked out of the lobby counting floor tiles.

In the car I thought about Mac Woo's link with the Nashua police. I opened my wallet and dug out Detective Remy Vachon's card. I hadn't spoken to him since the day we met at Henri's Motor Lodge, when he told me about losing the Dunn case. I called the number, expecting to get dumped into his voice mail.

To my surprise he answered, saying hello Dermot. He asked how the Dunn investigation was going. I gave him a summary and told him the reason for my call.

"I want to meet FBI agent Mac Woo," I said. "Can you make it happen?"

Vachon didn't answer right away. He probably paused to light his briar pipe.

"Why do you want to talk to Mac?"

"To ask him about the Boston FBI office. I want to know why Boston took the Dunn case away from the Bedford office."

I heard the striking of a match and the puffing of a pipe. Vachon could teach a seminar on delay tactics, if he ever got around to it. He said he'd call me back within the hour.

"I'm in Bedford," I said. "Should I stick around or go home?"

"Stick around," he said. Vachon called back an hour later. "Meet me tonight in Nashua at Milt's Piazza. It's a coffee shop in Clocktower Place. I'll be there at seven. Milt has a porch out back, lots of privacy, no one will bother us out there. I'll tell him to reserve it for us."

"What about Mac Woo?"

Vachon hung up.

23

AT SEVEN O'CLOCK I parked in front of Milt's Piazza, which was located in a restored riverfront building that once housed a cotton mill. I went inside and was promptly greeted by smiling Milt, who introduced himself with a vigorous handshake. I felt spoiled, being acknowledged in such a way. The only time someone extends a hand in Boston is when they're reaching for your credit card. Maybe I should move to New Hampshire. I thought about the hostile FBI receptionist from earlier in the day. She must be a Massachusetts transplant.

Milt led me to the back porch, the piazza he called it, which was enclosed with windows that afforded river views. Detective Remy Vachon was the only person there. He stood to greet me and then held up his briar pipe.

"Mind if I smoke?" he asked, striking a match.

He lit the bowl and blew a plume to the rafters. The scent lingered in the air like incense at a funeral Mass and reminded me of Glooscap's bulldog pipe. Vachon puffed and made me wait, waiting for what I didn't know. The prolonged pause wasn't a tactic, but his personality, his unhurried way of living. Maybe I *should* move to New Hampshire.

He sniffed the smoke with apparent joy, glanced at his watch and then at the door, which opened on cue. An Asian man came in. He was small in stature and had floppy gray hair, a man in his late forties or early fifties. I put my detecting skills to work and took a leap that he was Mac Woo.

He wore a rumpled suit that was ready for a Goodwill box. Lucky for him Don DeRosa wasn't here or he'd have been disrobed. His tie was loose and his eyes were tired. He didn't look like an FBI agent. He looked like a poet from Greenwich Village, just as Kenny said. He walked across the floor in a deliberate manner, careful not to step on a landmine. Vachon stood up and they embraced. The mutual respect was evident.

"Dermot, this is FBI agent Mac Woo," Vachon said.

Woo and I shook hands.

"Nice to meet you," Woo said. He sat in the chair next to me, near enough that I could see the circles under his eyes and the exhaustion on his face.

"Mac took the Dunn case from us in Nashua." Vachon began. "But it was more of a handoff on our part than a seizing on his. We agreed to work together on the investigation. As soon as Mac took control of the case, the Boston FBI took it from him, and in essence from me. I am not happy about it. Neither is Mac."

"The Boston FBI office used me," Woo added. "They knew Remy and I were close, and they knew he'd give me everything he had on the case. The FBI is supposed to cooperate with local law-enforcement. In that spirit, Remy and I agreed to cooperate, to work together on the Dunn murder. It never happened. Agent James Graham, through director Edmund O'Dwyer, appropriated the case from the Bedford office."

All this because of cigarette smuggling? Something else was going on.

"The Boston branch can seize a case from the local office?" I asked.

"They can and they did." Vachon answered for Woo. "The FBI's hierarchy is as rigid as the Catholic Church's."

"The FBI is a bowl of jello compared to the Catholic Church," I said.

"Bowl of jello or not, the FBI can be ruthless," Woo said. "They can destroy a man's life with the click of a computer key."

"It sounds like you've had experience." I waited for Woo to respond. He didn't. I moved ahead. "If Boston had the power to take the case, why didn't they simply take it from the start? Why did they drag you in as a go-between, Mac?"

"They knew the transition would go smoothly because of my friendship with Remy." Woo tapped his head with his forefinger. "And they wanted to get everything I knew up here. That's why they brought me in. Investigators always know more than what they put in their reports. I don't have to tell you how it works."

Woo removed a Marlboro from a soft pack and lit it with a Zippo. Vachon followed suit, relighting his pipe. Vachon nodded for Woo to continue.

"Before we talk about the Dunn murder, I'd like to talk about the Boston FBI," Woo said. "The shuffling of the Dunn case from Nashua to Bedford, and then from Bedford to Boston, is symptomatic of a larger problem that infects the Boston FBI office and therefore the entire New England region."

Jeez, Mac. I just want to solve a murder, not reform the federal government.

"Bear with me," Woo said. "I'll give you the broad picture."

He took a drag and shot a gray cylinder across the room that was as straight as a laser beam. Vachon followed with a stream from his pipe. Would they start a game of tic-tac-toe with the smoke? Woo walked to the bank of windows and cracked one open. A rush of smoke poured out and dissipated in the cold autumn air. Vachon joined Woo and whispered something to him. They returned to their chairs. Vachon racked his pipe in the ashtray. Woo crushed his cigarette in the same and started to talk.

"Remy and I will be giving you a data dump, which consists of an assortment of disparate facts for you to analyze. We've drawn our own inferences, of course, but the time has come for fresh eyes, fresh analysis."

"I assume you're talking about me." I thought about the scribble on my incident board in the hotel room. "You have high hopes."

No laughter, tough crowd.

"Eight years ago Dunn was arrested for armed robbery," Woo said. "James Graham was the arresting officer." He laughed with harshness. "I found this difficult to believe."

"Why?" I asked.

"Graham couldn't find a haystack in Texas, let alone a needle in it. The man is incapable of diagnosing evidence, and doubly incapable of drawing conclusions from it. Simply put, he's not smart enough. And on top of that he's lazy. And on top of being lazy, he's sloppy."

"You don't hold him in high regard," I said.

Again, no laughter.

"The Dunn collar fast-tracked Graham's teetering career," Woo said. "It also elevated Edmund O'Dwyer to an even higher level. The success they enjoyed earlier in their careers was reignited. They were stars again in the Bureau. Batman and Robin."

"I hear a 'but' coming."

"There is only one explanation for Graham's arrest of Dunn, and it wasn't investigative acumen," he said. "Somebody told him about Dunn's role in the robbery."

"An informer?" I guessed. "Someone close to Graham and O'Dwyer?"

"Most likely." Woo got up and stood by the windows again. "The armored car Dunn robbed was carrying three million in cash, not the six hundred thousand reported to the press."

"Making the prize that much more appetizing," I said. Nothing is ever as it seems in the annals of Charlestown crime. "Why did the bank lie about the amount stolen? Wouldn't it have slash the payout they got from the insurance claim?"

"It would and it did." Woo nodded. "I heard a rumor that a mobbed-up credit union in Rhode Island was laundering money through a Massachusetts concern, possibly another credit union in the Boston area."

"Rhode Island to Massachusetts, the crime crossed state lines," I said, thinking about the FBI. "Somebody told Vincent Dunn about the three million, somebody with inside information."

"I arrived at the same conclusion." Woo came back to his chair. "Vincent Dunn probably knew about the bonus money in the truck."

"And the money was never recovered." I thought about James Graham's lavish Wellesley estate, with the in-ground pool and the tennis court and the fancy cars in his double driveway. I thought about O'Dwyer's Weston mansion. The murder of Vincent Dunn closed the door on the armored-car incident. The heist money was in the wind. "Three million dollars," I said. "That's a pretty good motive for murder."

Vachon and Woo nodded.

24

MILT CAME INTO the piazza carrying a tray with a pot of coffee and all the paraphernalia that went with it. The three of us indulged in much needed caffeine. Vachon lit his pipe, Woo a Marlboro. I felt naked with nothing to suck on and wished I had a lollipop like Kojak. Woo turned to me.

"The connection between James Graham and Edmund O'Dwyer started long before the Dunn robbery." He tapped dead cinders into the ashtray. "They cut their teeth in Lowell, where they broke-up a gambling ring. This was twenty years ago."

"Gambling is a federal crime?" I asked.

"It is if it falls within the RICO statute," Woo said. "If racketeering is involved, or if the gambling crosses state lines, it becomes a federal crime and gives the FBI jurisdiction. O'Dwyer and Graham infiltrated the ring and brought it down."

"They had an informer," I said.

"Most likely," he said. "By the way, O'Dwyer is no genius, either."

"How did he get to the top?" I asked.

"Idiocy can be an asset in certain organizations. A useful moron is sometimes viewed more favorably than an intelligent researcher." Woo got back on track. "Graham was a rookie back then. O'Dwyer became his mentor and moved his career oafishly forward. I say oafishly because James Graham is a dolt. And now they're running the Boston office, that is to say, the entire New England region. But it began in Lowell twenty years ago."

Lowell again.

"Did the gambling ring have anything to do with Red McDermott?" I asked.

"What was that?" Vachon blinked. "You know about Red?"

"He was my father's friend. They served together in Vietnam."

Vachon seemed taken aback that I knew about Red.

"It was indeed McDermott's gambling ring," Vachon said. "He refused to play ball with Somerville and got killed for it. And now Dunn is dead, too."

"Are you saying the two killings are related?" I asked. "Dunn's and McDermott's?"

"Maybe," Vachon said. "Can I prove it? Not a chance."

"The killings happened twenty years apart," I said. "That must complicate things."

Both Vachon and Woo agreed.

"Vincent Dunn." Vachon pointed outside the window. "That's the Nashua River down below. Dunn could have floated by Milt's Piazza for all we know. If his body didn't get stuck in the weeds downstream, he might have floated to the Merrimack River and out to sea."

I shook my head.

"He'd have got hung up in Lowell at the Pawtucket Gatehouse." I went to the windows and looked at the stagnant water. If you dropped a champagne cork in it tonight, it would be in the same spot in the morning. "No way Dunn gets as far as Lowell."

"You're probably right." Vachon allowed. "What I'm getting at is this. If he didn't get tangled up at the bend, we might not have found him at all."

They'd have found him.

"Back to McDermott," I said to Vachon. "You work in Nashua, New Hampshire. Why do you know so much about Red if he was killed in Lowell, Massachusetts?"

Vachon examined his pipe, happy for the question.

"Red branched out to Nashua. That's the reason I got involved. I had just made detective, and Nashua appointed me liaison to the Middlesex County DA's office in Massachusetts. The appointment was a big deal for me. I was young and idealistic, about your age, when I still thought I could make a difference. We were making quick headway on Red's murder when the FBI ruined things."

"Are you saying the FBI had something to do with Red's death?" I asked.

"No, I'm not saying that. In my opinion, Red's murder was mob related. He didn't pay the piper, as the saying goes. You have to pay to play in Boston."

"The thug's vig," I said. "You pay or they send a leg breaker."

"Or a killer."

Vachon was right about the killer.

"So you worked with Middlesex County," I said.

"And the Massachusetts state police. They had a top investigator. I'm blanking on his name at the moment. It was twenty years ago. The guy's probably dead now. Was it Shears? Anyway, the Boston FBI took the McDermott case from Shears, and they convicted a Haverhill man, a three-time loser named Vegas DePena. The conviction was a joke in my judgement. And then DePena died in prison."

Convenient, DePena's death. I thought about what Vachon said, that Red had expanded into New Hampshire.

"What about the New Hampshire state police?" I asked. "Did they get involved?"

"A trooper named Leo Raymond was assigned to the case. He did some excellent work with Massachusetts, and then—"

"And then the Boston FBI came along." I made a mental note to ask Captain Raymond the name of the Massachusetts state trooper. I turned to Mac Woo. "What can you tell me about agent Emma Hague?"

Woo smiled for the first time. I didn't know he could.

"Emma is ambitious beyond ambitious," he said. "She started out in the art-theft squad, but you already know about that."

I grunted. Woo continued.

"Emma was credited with solving a decades-old art-museum robbery, which she solved with your help. Emma is more intelligent than Graham, I suppose everyone is, but she wasn't smart enough to crack the museum case. The truth is she didn't figure out a thing. You did."

"She'd have gotten it eventually."

"I disagree," Woo said. "I'm not berating Emma when I say that, nor am I berating the art-theft squad. They investigated that particular robbery for twenty years and came up with zilch. And then you came along." Woo eyeballed the Marlboros so lustfully I wanted to smoke one myself. He shook one loose and lit it. "Emma is an enigma. On the one hand her motives are transparent, to claw her way to the top of the Bureau. On the other hand, she is calculating. Emma is not without guile."

"You should be a profiler," I said.

"Are you working with her on the Dunn murder?" Woo asked. "I heard some rumblings."

"I am, sort of," I said.

"Watch your back." Woo warned. "Emma won't set out to betray you, but if an opportunity comes along to bump her career, she'll leave you gawking."

"Noted," I said. *She already left me gawking once.* "Does the name Tony Cedrone mean anything to either of you?"

Vachon took this one.

"He was a person of interest in the McDermott murder. Cedrone had a beef with Red because Red refused to pay the vig, to use your word. The Massachusetts state trooper I was telling you about earlier, he was convinced Cedrone killed McDermott."

"And then the FBI arrested Vegas DePena for it," I said. "Do you think the FBI was protecting Cedrone?"

"Some of us thought so, and some of us *knew* so," Vachon said. "Leo Raymond sure knew so. Raymond got so angry he told the Boston FBI what he suspected."

"What did the Boston FBI think about that?"

"They thought Raymond should stay in New Hampshire." Vachon turned to Woo. "Show Dermot the pictures, Mac."

Woo took a folder from his briefcase and handed it to me. I emptied the contents on the table, a pile of photos that showed James Graham, Edmund O'Dwyer, and Tony Cedrone with political muckety-mucks and known thugs. The pictures were taken at various locations around Greater Boston, and they were taken over the course of many years. Some of the men in the photos were dead. Did Woo take the photos himself? It didn't seem possible.

"Where did you get these?"

"I took most of them myself," Woo said. "Some of them were in a research folder at Boston headquarters. I snuck them out the day I was transferred up here. As for the pictures I took, I used a thirty-five millimeter camera, one of those vintage jobs that use Kodachrome film."

"Why a film camera?" I asked.

"I didn't want to risk a digital camera getting hacked," he said. "And I didn't trust anyone to develop the film. I built a dark room in my cellar and developed the rolls myself."

I went through the photos again and was treated to a pictorial history of Boston organized crime in the new millennium.

"There's enough evidence here to put away O'Dwyer and Graham for decades," I said. "What are you waiting for?"

"It's not evidence, it's data. The photos don't prove anything in themselves. At best they're circumstantial." Woo held up a picture of Graham and Cedrone in front of a church. "They could be going to a christening."

The christening in *The Godfather*.

"If they're useless, why show them to me?" I asked.

"I didn't say they were useless. I said they were circumstantial. They won't put anyone in jail, and they won't get you an indictment. Think of them as supplemental material, as icing on a solid case."

I handed them back to Woo.

"Keep them," he said. "Don't tell anybody where you got them. I still have thirty-eight days until I retire."

"You're taking a chance giving them to me."

"I know I am," Woo said, but he didn't seem concerned.

"How about Dez Barry from Charlestown?" I asked them. "Ring any bells?"

"His name came up in Dunn's armored-car case," Vachon said, tapping his pipe in the ashtray. "A reliable source told me that Dez was in on the job with Dunn. Dunn never said a word about him."

"I'm not surprised," I said. "Ever hear the name Collings or Grace Collins?"

They both said no.

"How about Eddie Loan?"

They didn't know Eddie, either. I was about to leave when another question popped into my head, this one for Woo.

"Graham spent two hours at the Bedford FBI office yesterday. Why was he there?"

"I didn't know he *was* there." Woo looked surprised. "I wonder what he was doing?"

"He didn't come to see you?"

"Me? Persona non grata?" Woo said. "I've been relegated to back-office chores that a trained monkey could do. I'm hanging on until my pension kicks in." He looked at his cellphone. "Which happens in thirty-eight days, four hours and eleven minutes."

What a waste of talent.

I started to get up.

"Before you go," Woo said, "I want to show you one more thing." He removed a single sheet of paper from his briefcase. "The FBI uses a diagnostic tool called DIOG, which is short for Domestic Investigations and Operations Guide."

"That clarifies things."

"In layman's terms it's a flowchart of a crime, or in this case, crimes." Woo held up the paper. "I dumbed it down so it's simpler to understand."

"Thanks."

I looked at the chart and saw three boxes side-by-side. The left box said Red McDermott murder, the middle one said Vincent Dunn armored-car conviction, the right one said Vincent Dunn murder.

"Can you explain it?" I asked.

"I entered the data from all three crimes into DIOG," he said. "I entered the people, the locations, the time frames, et cetera."

"And?"

"The program showed a ninety-two percent chance the three crimes are connected. Two people were heavily involved in all three, Edmund O'Dwyer and James Graham. O'Dwyer and Graham manipulated the cases to gain control of them." He put the flowchart back in the bag and snapped the buckle. "There's a third man I didn't factor into the chart."

"Tony Cedrone," I said.

"Correct, Tony Cedrone," Woo said. "When I added Cedrone's name into DIOG, the number jumped to ninety-nine percent."

"I'd call that a statistically significant connection," I said, showing off my deductive skills. They didn't seem impressed.

Mac Woo had presented the data and the conclusions the data suggested. But the whole thing felt sterile to me, like the jargon we hear from front-office baseball geeks. I wanted to hear from a bush-league scout who'd been forgotten by the big club, a circumstance that Mac knew all too well. I wanted Mac's gut reaction to the stuff, and so I asked him if he had gleaned any insights from the data. He became energized.

"I have indeed speculated on the data," he said, "and since

it is speculation, I urge you to be skeptical yourself." He got to his feet and bowed his head like a college professor getting ready to make a key point. "I concluded that Edmund O'Dwyer, James Graham, and Tony Cedrone are a criminal enterprise unto themselves, a thuggish troika that controls all the illicit business in New England: sports gambling, the sex trade, drugs, guns, you name it."

"Tony Cedrone can't control his temper," I said. "How could he control New England?"

"He does it with the help of the Boston FBI," Woo said. "The Boston FBI gives him cover. Remember, I'm speculating. But I believe Cedrone is on par with his FBI counterparts."

"You think he's on equal footing with the FBI?" I asked.

"O'Dwyer and Graham took care of everything for Cedrone." Woo continued. "They dismantled the gangland hierarchy in Boston, and they did it with Cedrone's help. Think about it. All the big players are gone. Maddog Madden is doing life in federal pen. Sonny Solomon went away. Harry the Hat disappeared."

"I forgot those names."

"The FBI put them away, or chased them away, and cleared a path to the top for Tony Cedrone. Tony filled the void they left behind."

"Unbelievable," I said. "If the Boston FBI is partnering with Tony, the money coming in must be mindboggling."

"Narcotics, ghost guns, prostitution, kiddie porn—anything you want in the sex trade. The money is beyond mindboggling." Woo shoved his hands into his pockets and looked at the floor. "Have you noticed there have been no major mob arrests in the last ten years?"

"I haven't been following it," I said. "Are you saying the arrests ended when Cedrone took over?"

"In essence, yes, the arrests stopped. If the Boston FBI makes a mob-related arrest these days, they're arresting someone who presents a threat Cedrone's power. Tony runs things, carte blanche, courtesy of the O'Dwyer and Graham." Woo stopped talking and sat in his chair, lit a fresh cigarette and looked at me. "But remember what I said earlier. Everything I told you here is pure conjecture."

"Conjecture based on facts," I said.

Woo and Vachon nodded.

"That's good enough for me," I said.

25

I WOKE UP feeling washed out from Milt's Piazza. The smell of burnt tobacco still lingered in my nostrils. Vachon and Woo had thrown a lot at me, and I needed time to sort it out. I sat up in bed and looked outside and saw a heartless sky. The rain clouds triggered a dull shiver inside me, and the shiver led to an annoying irritability. I wanted to pull down the shade and pull the covers over my head. As Aretha Franklin sang it: 'Without a warning, the blues walked in this morning.'

Self-pity is dangerous territory for an alkie like me. It can lead to a drink. I didn't want to go back to that life of misery, where each day was like a two-hundred-meter dash, beginning with a staggered start and ending with a desperate lunge for the finish line. I needed a meeting fast. I checked the AA meeting-list book and found one nearby on Washington Street.

After the meeting I walked back to the hotel with a better attitude. I had an espresso with Al Barese in the trattoria, and we talked about Boston College football. Al yearned for the glory days of Doug Flutie, days that took place years before my time. He recounted how BC beat the best teams in the nation with Flutie at the controls.

"They defeated Penn State when Paterno was there, Alabama twice, Texas A&M twice, North Carolina, Miami, Syracuse.

Clemson, too. During a twenty-one-game span, Clemson had one loss and one tie, both to Doug Flutie."

The sports talk further boosted my mood.

I went to my room and called Kenny Bowen and asked him if he'd like to meet tomorrow for a workout. He said yes and added, "Harold Schmidt will be there."

"The name sounds familiar."

"He medaled in the hammer throw at the London Olympics. Come at noon."

"Can't wait," I said, and hung up.

I hadn't put down my cell phone when the house phone rang. It was Vito the concierge, who said, "Mr. Sparhawk, there's a woman at the front desk who'd like to speak to you. She won't give a name."

"Is she good-looking?"

"Depends on your taste, sir."

"I was kidding. I'm on my way."

I walked to the lobby.

Vito pointed to a woman who was dressed in a finely tailored blue suit that must have cost her a week's pay, if she in fact worked. Whatever happened to off-the-rack? And why did I care? Her black hair was styled in a short bob, and her face was pleasing in a wholesome way, perfect for an apple pie ad. She wore no jewelry. Maybe she spent all her money on the suit.

I told her I was Dermot Sparhawk. She said her name was Susan Pike. So far, so good. She asked if we could go to a private place to talk, and I suggested the hotel trattoria. We sat at a table in the corner.

"I work for the U.S. Attorney's office in Boston," she said. "I report directly to Maddy Savitz, whom you know."

"Maddy and I worked together on a case a few years ago."

"She told me you solved it."

"Team effort," I said. "Would you like an espresso or a cappuccino?"

"Thank you, that sounds good."

"Let's sit at the cafe bar," I said. "The Hotel Abruzzi makes the best cappuccino in the city. Follow me."

We got up from the table and went to the bar. Benny Venuti watched us go by, keeping a close eye on Susan Pike. Was he worried she was an assassin?

"Is he your friend?" she asked.

"My bodyguard."

"You don't look like you need a bodyguard."

The cafe bar had three stools, all unoccupied. We sat with a stool between us and ordered cappuccinos from a matronly barista, who prepared the machine and pushed a button. The milk frother hissed and sputtered to a stop, and the barista placed the foamy cups in front of us. I had a sip and waited for Susan Pike to speak.

"U.S. Attorney Savitz wants to meet with you."

"Why didn't she simply call me?" I asked. "I don't need a special invitation."

"Ms. Savitz sent me to explain the situation." She drank her cappuccino. "Wow, this is very tasty."

"Explain what situation?" I asked.

"She wants me to drive you to meet her," she said.

The whole scene was getting mysterious, but mystery went with the job.

"Let's go." I got off the stool. "Let's go see Maddy."

"Not now, tomorrow."

"Tomorrow is Saturday." Now it *was* mysterious. "No offense, Ms. Pike, but I'd like to see your ID."

"Of course."

She opened her bag and showed me a federal badge and an official-looking ID that said Susan Pike, Assistant U.S. Attorney, Massachusetts. The badge and ID looked valid enough, but for all I knew I she bought them at a schlock shop on Route 1 in Saugus.

"I will pick you up at seven in the morning in front of the hotel." She blinked her eyes. "Will you be ready?"

"I'll be waiting with a cappuccino for you," I said. "Before you go. How did you know I was staying at the Hotel Abruzzi?"

"Ms. Savitz will answer all your questions tomorrow," she said. "Please don't mention this meeting to anybody, Mr. Sparhawk."

Susan Pike left the trattoria. I finished my frothy drink and walked past Benny Venuti, who said, "The one who got away. You can't win 'em all, Sparhawk."

26

AT SEVEN IN the morning Susan Pike picked me in front of the hotel. I got into the front seat and handed her a cup of cappuccino, which she crammed into a cup holder. She placed both hands on the steering wheel like a driver-ed student, pulled away from the curb after checking the rearview mirror, and took the expressway north into the O'Neill Tunnel, staying below the speed limit. We went by the first exit. I'd expected her take that exit for the federal courthouse, but she didn't. She kept driving north.

"We're not going to Maddy's office?" I asked.

"That is correct, Mr. Sparhawk."

"Call me Dermot and tell me where we're going."

"We're meeting Ms. Savitz at a location she deemed safe."

She bypassed the question as smoothly as she'd bypassed the courthouse exit.

She ramped out of the O'Neill Tunnel and merged onto Storrow Drive and drove along the Charles River, going past Kenmore Square and Boston University. Storrow Drive became Soldier Field Road at Harvard Stadium, and Soldier Field Road became Nonantum Street in Newton. My father once told me that Nonantum was Micmac for blessing. We'll see.

She drove into an empty parking lot and stopped at a wooden building, a shack really, which abutted the Charles River. Floating in front of the building was a battered, waterlogged wharf. I wondered if Noah moored his ark there when the Great Flood receded.

We went inside to find a boathouse with sculls and oars hanging on the walls. The scant daylight that lit the place came from a row of grimy transom windows under the eaves. No one could see in, no one could see out. A space heater neutralized the cold, but barely.

On the table I saw a Box O' Joe from Dunkin' Donuts and a platter of honey-glazed crullers. They knew I was coming. That's not all that awaited me. U.S. Attorney Maddy Savitz, FBI agent Emma Hague, and FBI agent Mac Woo were also at the table. How did they get here? I saw no cars in the lot. Susan Pike left the boathouse.

"Thanks for joining us today," Maddy said. Her light brown hair reached beyond her shoulders, and her lithe body formed perfectly to the chair. "I apologize for bringing you here in secret. We couldn't risk meeting in my office. Word would have leaked out."

"It always does," I said, walking to the coffee box. I poured a cup and grabbed a cruller. "I assume we're here to talk about the Vincent Dunn case."

"We'll get to that," Maddy said. "First, we need to talk about a more pressing matter. The Boston FBI filed a lawsuit against you. My office received the complaint yesterday."

"For what?"

"For tampering with an ongoing federal investigation," she said.

"What investigation?"

"Easy, Dermot," Maddy said.

Emma Hague spoke next, addressing me like an out-and-out stranger. I liked it better when she was undressing me like an out-and-out sex object.

"I told Ms. Savitz about my suspicions regarding Edmund O'Dwyer and James Graham and their management of the Boston FBI office," Emma said. "I told her about the Vincent Dunn murder investigation, and how the Boston FBI usurped it from the

New Hampshire office. I also told Ms. Savitz that you were looking into the Dunn murder, and that O'Dwyer and Graham might take exception to that."

Usurped?

"I put two and two together," Maddy said. "When I received the FBI complaint against you, I remembered what Emma told me about Boston. And, of course, I know you personally."

Mac Woo cleared his throat. It was his turn.

"Ms. Savitz assigned me liaison to her office, sub rosa," Mac said. "I am using vacation time while I serve in this capacity. Out of sight, out of mind. Nobody in the New Hampshire office will miss me if I'm on vacation. I'm hoping to throw O'Dwyer and Graham off the scent."

"Congrats, Mac."

"It feels good to be back in action," he said. The dark circles around his eyes were gone. His energy level was spiking. "According to the Boston FBI warrant application, you meddled in the Dunn case, just as Ms. Savitz stated."

"I'm a private eye," I said. "I meddle."

Mac shook his head.

"This is bad news, Dermot. If Ms. Savitz approves the application, the FBI will ruin your life. You'll be in and out of court for the next five years, and so will your lawyers, piling up a mountain of billable hours."

"Jesus." I placed my cup on the table and sat with them. Maddy handed it back to me and said, "Drink your coffee, Dermot. I'm not going to sign the request right away."

"Thanks, I think."

"I will lead the FBI into *believing* I'm signing off." Maddy grinned, enjoying the fiasco. It wasn't her head on the block. "I sent O'Dwyer a note telling him I'd be moving ahead on the FBI's request when I returned from vacation. That will appease them for a while."

Maddy could have told me this over the phone. Something more was coming. Mac Woo laid it out for me.

"At the behest of Ms. Savitz, the FBI's internal affairs division in Washington is opening a case against the Boston FBI, naming O'Dwyer and Graham as defendants. As liaison to Ms. Savitz, I will manage all communications between FBI headquarters in D.C. and the U.S. Attorney's Office in Boston. Agent Hague will be my source in the Boston FBI. Ms. Hague reports to me. I report to Ms. Savitz."

I smiled to myself. Maddy Savitz pulled a double switch, to use baseball parlance. The Boston FBI filed with her against me. She convinced Washington to file against Boston for her.

"Too dangerous for Emma," I said. "O'Dwyer will figure it out."

"I can handle Edmund O'Dwyer," Emma answered back, stuffing me like a putz. On top of that, she did an amazing job concealing her lust for me, so amazing you'd think she had no interest in me at all. She continued. "And James Graham is so dumb he can't figure out how to turn right on red."

I have trouble with that myself.

"I don't like it," I said, but dropped it. "Where do I come in?"

"Keep doing what you're doing," Maddy said. "Keep digging on Vincent Dunn, and keep Emma up to date."

"How long can you postpone the lawsuit against me?" I asked.

"For a week," she said. "I'm on my way to Nantucket for vacation."

"Nantucket in the late fall?" I asked.

"No one will be there to bother me," she said. "Just the way I like it." She stood up from the table. "That's all I have."

One thing struck me odd as we were leaving the boathouse. Mac Woo never talked about Tony Cedrone. He never mentioned Cedrone's connection to O'Dwyer and Graham. At Milt's Piazza, Mac laid out a credible theory that Cedrone was in league with the Boston FBI. But as soon as he said it he backed off, saying it was conjecture. Mac must be playing safe. Underlings with bright ideas are often punted to the sidelines. Mac had eaten enough crow during his career. He kept his mouth shut.

Outside near the riverbank I asked Maddy, "Why did you pick this place to meet?"

"I grew up in Nonantum, just over the hill," she said, pointing. "I rowed here summers as a teenager, and I continued rowing in college on the crew team. I belong to a different club now, down river by the universities, but I still have the keys to this place. You should consider sculling, Dermot. With your long arms you'd be a natural, *and* it is great exercise."

"Indians paddle canoes."

"Ha-ha-ha." She deadpanned.

A black SUV pulled into the lot and picked up the Savitz-Hague-Woo trio. Susan Pike waited for me in her idling vehicle.

Why did I feel like I was getting conned?

27

SUSAN PIKE DROPPED me at the hotel. I went in and found the lobby empty. I saw no sign of Al and Andy Barese and no sign of the Benny and the Venuti brothers. Vito the concierge was busy on the phone. He looked up and nodded to me. All was well. I looked at my cellphone. Ten o'clock, plenty of time. I was scheduled to meet Kenny at Harvard Stadium for a workout at noon.

I went to my room and sat at the window facing Washington Street. A male and a female cardinal were perched on a utility wire across the street. The females are brownish-red, not brilliant red like their males counterparts. They flew off together and soared out of sight, probably to make little cardinals, also known as bishops.

My cell phone rang. The caller ID said POTENTIAL SPAM, practically screaming it at me. I answered it anyway. A man with a raspy voice and a surly attitude said, "Quit the Dunn case, Sparhawk. Quit lookin' into the murder. This is your last warning."

I couldn't remember getting a first warning

Threat issued, he hung up. I went back to watching Washington Street. A Silver Line bus came along, with its accordion middle and sleek chromium siding. It reminded me of an Airstream camper. It drove in the designated bus lane and slowed to a stop.

The doors opened with a pneumatic whoosh and six passengers got off.

The phone rang again from POTENIAL SPAM. Maybe I should add him to my contacts list. I answered it and waited for the next threat. Raspy must have popped a cough drop, because the hoarseness was gone.

"I hope I'm not disturbing you, Dermot," the man said. "This is Detective Vachon."

"You came up as potential spam."

"I'm using a burner phone," he said, but didn't say why. "When we met at Milt's Piazza, I told you about a Massachusetts state trooper I worked with on the McDermott murder. I said his name was Shears. It was Spear, Lieutenant Chuck Spear."

Why, after twenty years, does Red McDermott's name keep coming up?

"You think Red's murder is connected to Dunn's," I said. "Mac Woo thought so, too. I'm working on the Dunn case, Detective. And I'm nowhere close to solving it. Tell me why I should invest time in Red McDermott."

"Red is the key to solving Dunn," he said. "Just talk to Spear. He's retired now and has plenty of time on his hands. I told him you'd be calling."

Vachon texted me the number. I dialed it and an older man answered. I asked for Lieutenant Chuck Spear.

"I'm Chuck Spear," he said.

I told him my name and why I was calling, to ask him about Red McDermott's murder. I also told him about Detective Vachon's call to me.

"Remy said you'd be calling," Spear said. "I'd be glad to talk to you, but I'd rather talk in person. Phones these days, I don't trust them."

"That's fine with me, Lieutenant."

"Are you free tomorrow?"

"Yup."

"Meet me a Dillon's Local in Plymouth," he said. "I'll be there at two o'clock. It's quieter after the lunch crowd goes away."

He gave me the address. I told him I'd be there tomorrow at two.

I put on my sweats to meet Kenny Bowen at Harvard Stadium. Today we'd be working out with Olympic hammer thrower Harold Schmidt, who'd been a track and field star at Iowa State. So far it's been a day of S's: Savitz, Spear, Schmidt, and Surly-voice. My brain works that way, looking for patterns no matter how trivial they might be.

No wonder the case wasn't solved.

28

I WAS DRIVING west on Memorial Drive to meet Kenny when I sensed somebody following me. A glance in the rearview mirror confirmed it. I usually don't notice such things. That's Harraseeket Kid's department. I took an indirect route, taking the Western Avenue Bridge over the Charles River into the Allston-Brighton neighborhood. Nobody in Boston knows where Allston ends and Brighton begins. A friend once told me that the visiting side of Harvard Stadium was in Allston and the home side was in Brighton. I believed him, until he started laughing.

I meandered on side roads. The tracker meandered with me. On North Harvard Street, in either Allston or Brighton, I parked across from the stadium and got out of the car. The tracker, driving a dark SUV, sailed past me toward the Charles. I jotted down the registration number. It seemed too easy. I was surprised the driver didn't wave to me going by, the rude bastard.

Kenny was waiting for me at the gate. His shorn head took on the color of the overcast sky, and his Dartmouth Big Green track suit darkened to black-green on this sunless afternoon.

"Harold's at the hammer circle," he said. "He's one of the best in the world."

We cut through the concourse of the stadium to the back field to watch Harold Schmidt, a blond-haired behemoth with feet the size of scuba fins. He was wearing an Iowa State Cyclones sweat suit, dark red with gold lettering.

"Someone followed me here," I said to Kenny. "I got the plate."

"Maybe it was Ruth Greenberg." Kenny smiled. "I'm kidding, of course, but not about her interest in you. What's the number?"

I handed him an index card with the registration on it.

"It's funny you said it was Ruth," I said.

"I was kidding, Dermot."

"Because I thought a woman following me. When I changed lanes on Memorial Drive, the car signaled to stay behind me. How many thugs signal when they're tailing somebody?"

"Interesting," Kenny said. "He's stepping into the circle."

Harold did a few prep swings, moving the hammer in easy arcs above his head, keeping his arms straight and his torso perpendicular. He went into an accelerating spin and delivered the hammer into the air. The steel ball landed with a thud, leaving the biggest divot since the Stooges swung golf clubs.

"Was that beautiful or what?" Kenny said. "That's why Harold is the hammer king."

"Yep, he's a stud."

Harold wiped his hands on a towel and jogged to retrieve the hammer.

"Harold wants to see the North End," Kenny said. "Can we postpone our workout?"

I couldn't say yes fast enough.

"Why don't you join us?" he said. "We're going to Beneventos on Salem Street. The marinara sauce is out of this world."

"Can't, I'm busy."

I told Kenny about Chuck Spear, the retired state police lieutenant. I told him about the raspy-voiced man who threatened me to drop the case. I told him about the meeting with Maddy Savitz, Emma Hague, and Mac Woo at the boathouse, and how the Boston FBI had filed a case against me for meddling in the Dunn investigation, and how the Washington FBI was filing a case against the Boston FBI for possible corruption.

"You *have* been busy," he said. "I'll look into Chuck Spear."

"I'm meeting him tomorrow."

"Let's meet here the day after at noon," he said. "I'll tell you what I found out. And we'll pump iron under the stadium."

My back ached thinking about it. Kenny's workouts consisted of core exercises. Squats, cleans, deadlifts. I could already feel my tendons popping.

"One other thing," Kenny said. "I'm worried about the raspy-voiced man. Don't leave yourself vulnerable. Ask Harraseeket Kid to work with you."

"I have the Venuti brothers."

"They're at the hotel. Most of the time you're not at the hotel. Call Kid."

Kenny made a good point about the possible threat from man with raspy voice. I made a mental note to call Kid.

29

THE NEXT DAY I began my pilgrimage to Plymouth to meet Lt. Chuck Spear. At the Braintree split I stayed left for Route 3, keeping an eye on the rearview mirror.

Sure enough, a dark SUV stayed with me. Three hundred thousand cars a day navigated the split, and I bet a good percentage of them were dark SUVs. I got off at Union Street in Braintree and pulled into a gas station. The SUV exited too, but drove by me. I topped off the tank to kill time. The SUV didn't return. Instead of getting back on the highway, which was easy pickings for a spy, I took Route 3A south, the slow road to Plymouth. The Mayflower got there faster from England.

I parked in front of Dillon's Local restaurant, the rendezvous spot. On the left side of the entrance flew an American flag, on the right an Irish one. I went in. An older man with a bald head tore himself away from a crock of French onion soup and looked at me. He was sitting at a widow table by himself. I took a guess.

"Lieutenant Spear," I said to him. "Thanks for making the time."

"My wife is down the Cape visiting her sister. I have plenty of time." He held up a folder. "The McDermott file. I revisited it last night."

Spear stood up and we shook hands and sat at the table. He put on his reading glasses and thumbed through the pages. I looked outside at the icy gray waters of Plymouth Harbor. Spear closed the folder.

"Are you still there, Sparhawk?" he asked. "Zoned out?"

"Sorry, daydreaming."

"The ocean will do that to you, it'll put you in a trance." He went back to his soup. "What do you want to know?"

"Vachon told me you headed the McDermott investigation."

"I did," he said. "I reported to a captain, but I led it."

"Did you work with an FBI agent named Mac Woo?"

"You've done your homework," Spear said. "I worked briefly with Woo. The higher-ups yanked him off the case early on. Then they yanked us off it, us being the state police."

"I talked to Mac Woo in Nashua," I said. "Remy Vachon, too. I talked to them about the Vincent Dunn murder."

"Vachon mentioned Dunn."

"Woo and Vachon told me about McDermott. The Boston FBI took the McDermott case from Middlesex County twenty years ago. They took the Dunn case from Nashua last week. Talk to me about McDermott."

Spear pushed away the empty crock and wiped his mouth with a paper napkin.

"The McDermott case turned on a compelling piece of evidence, the murder weapon, a Glock nine. The gun belonged to three-time loser named Vegas DePena."

"How did you find it?"

"A woman with a Spanish accent called the hotline. She said DePena killed McDermott over a gambling debt. McDermott supposedly owed DePena money."

"Supposedly?"

"McDermott never welched," Spear said. "He paid his losses the way good bookies do."

"Do you think the woman was lying?"

"It's possible," he said. "A judge issued a search warrant. We raided DePena's apartment and found the gun tucked under a couch cushion. Ballistics confirmed it was gun that killed Red McDermott."

"Under a cushion?" Nobody is that dumb. "What about Tony Cedrone?"

"You *have* done your homework. At first I thought Cedrone murdered McDermott, but then we found the murder weapon." He shrugged. "What could we do? We had to go with the physical evidence. DePena was a known criminal. Violent, too. He assaulted a store clerk during a robbery and put the lady in a coma. For a lousy two hundred bucks he fractured her skull."

"I'm not saying DePena should be venerated. I'm asking if he murdered McDermott."

"The evidence says he did it."

The evidence said it, but Spear didn't seem convinced.

"That hotline tip was mighty convenient," I said. "Finding the murder weapon was even more convenient."

"I agree it was convenient." Spear shrugged again. His body language said he didn't buy the chain of events. "Sometimes you get lucky."

And sometimes the fix is in.

"Why didn't DePena dump the gun?" I asked.

"I don't know."

"What if the Boston FBI planted it?" I said. "What if they framed DePena?"

"I thought the same thing, but another piece of evidence came in that sealed it for me," he said. "We tracked down the man who sold DePena the gun. He copped to a plea in exchange for a lenient sentence."

"Did the Spanish lady call the hotline on that one, too?"

He ignored me.

"DePena didn't deny buying the gun," he said. "He didn't deny killing McDermott. His lawyer, a shyster named LaPaz, didn't dispute the charges. He never offered a defense. They took the deal, case closed."

"It never went to trial?"

"No trial," he said. "I initially liked Cedrone for McDermott's murder, but DePena more or less confessed to it. He was sentenced to life, and we stopped looking at Cedrone."

"I can see why."

"In the end it didn't matter. DePena died six months later of pancreatic cancer. The poor bastard withered away to nothing in the prison infirmary at Souza-Baranowski."

"What a way to go, dying alone in prison."

Everything fit together, nice and neat. DePena goes down for McDermott's murder, DePena is dead six months later, and Cedrone skates unscathed.

"Do you remember the name of the gun dealer?" I asked.

Spear checked the file.

"Ronald Campbell," he said. "Jamaica Plain."

"Where I can find him?"

"Forest Hills Cemetery," he answered. "If you dig him up, he'll have two bullet holes in his head."

"Tony Cedrone."

"My thought, too."

"What about DePena's family?" I asked. "Is it worth talking to them?"

"Who knows?" He looked at his notes. "DePena had a wife named Rosaria. She lived in Haverhill at the time. Don't know if she's still there. They had an infant son named Diego. The kid grew up without a father, but he would have anyway. DePena was sick."

"I'll check out the family."

"You're probably wasting your time," he said.

"I'm an expert at wasting time," I said. "Besides, it'll give me something to do."

"I'm a phone call away if you need anything."

"Thanks, Lieutenant." I got up. "Is it okay if I borrow the McDermott file?"

"I guess so." He handed it to me. "Make sure you give it back. I don't want it floating around in the public. It's an official document."

"I'll return it."

We shook hands and I went out to my car.

30

BEFORE I LEFT Plymouth, I called Buckley Louis and asked him to find the address of Rosaria DePena, originally from Haverhill. I told him I wasn't sure if she still lived in Haverhill. For that matter I wasn't sure if she was still alive. He said he'd get on it and call me back. I grabbed a cup of coffee and drove to Plymouth harbor and waited. It made no sense to drive somewhere until I knew where I was going.

Buckley called and said that Rosaria still lived in Haverhill. He texted me the address. I entered it into the GPS and a map appeared with a florescent blue line, the route. Haverhill was a straight shot north from Plymouth, so straight it could have been a longitude line.

I merged onto Route 3 and began my journey to yet another Merrimack Valley mill town. Ninety minutes later I pulled into Haverhill, the Queen Slipper City, according to a welcome sign sponsored by the mayor.

Rosaria DePena's house was located just off Route 110 near the Merrimack River. It was an older house but well maintained. The porch was level, the shutters were square, and the siding was freshly painted. I rang the doorbell. A stocky woman in her mid-forties answered. I introduced myself with a smile, handed her my card, and asked her if she was Rosaria DePena.

"My name is Rosaria Cabral now," she said. "I got married again last month."

"Congratulations," I said.

She looked at me like I was an idiot and asked what I wanted.

"I'm looking into the murder of Red McDermott." I explained. "I'd like to ask you a few questions about your former husband Vegas."

"Vegas is dead." She hugged herself with both arms. "Twenty years he is dead."

"I know he's dead," I said. "I'm familiar with the case."

"You are disrespectful."

"I apologize, Ms. Cabral. I just wanted to ask you—"

"Leave," she said. "Go away or I will call the police."

"I just wanted to--"

She rightly closed the door in my face.

I went to my car and drove back to Charlestown. I wanted to talk to Buckley Louis, who was waiting in our Navy Yard office, if I ever got there. The traffic slowed to a crawl in Woburn and came to a standstill in Medford. I clicked onWBZ for a traffic report. A truck with a high load got stuck under an overpass. The state police had closed three lanes, leaving one open. I scooted off I-93 and took backroads into the city.

By the time I got to Charlestown the skies were dark, but the lights were burning in the office, making me feel like I was home. I couldn't wait to get inside. I went through the door and saw Buckley typing on his computer and Harraseeket Kid reading a newspaper at the conference table. Neither of them looked up to acknowledge me, which oddly enough made me feel that much more at home. No special welcome was needed. I poured a cup of coffee and sat with Kid, who said, "I love reading the obituaries. The writers give you a mini biography of the dead."

"Unless the dead man was a murder victim like Vincent Dunn," I said. "Then the bios on the front page."

He folded the paper and tossed it on a chair. Buckley turned off the monitor and removed his horn-rimmed reading glasses. I was about to bring them up to speed, when a young Hispanic man flung open the door and barged in.

"Which one of you is Sparhawk?" he snapped, speaking with no accent. He was about twenty years old, small in stature and volcanic with anger. He was wearing oil-stained coveralls, and his work boots were caked with grease. "I asked a question. Which one of you is—"

"I'm Sparhawk," I said, standing up. I allow no man to encroach on my space issuing threats. I looked at his hands. No weapons, unless he had an assassin's stiletto up his sleeve. Kid was standing next to me, his hand on the Bowie knife. The man came forward and practically stepped on my toes. I couldn't help but respect his courage. His head came up to my chest.

"You scared the shit out'a my mother, Sparhawk," he said. "She called me crying."

Rosaria.

"You must be Diego DePena, Vegas's son," I said. "I apologize for scaring your mother. I wanted to ask her about your father."

Diego paused before he spoke, not a bad practice.

"My father died twenty years ago. Why are you harassing my mother about him now?"

"I'm investigating the murder of a man named Vincent Dunn." I told him. "He was killed in Nashua. The case has similarities to the McDermott murder."

"Yeah, right. Red McDermott." He snorted. "The man my father supposedly killed, even though he didn't."

"Pour yourself a coffee." I pointed to the counter. "Relax, pour a cup and sit down with us. We're on your side."

To my surprise he did. He poured a cup and sat next to Harraseeket Kid. Buckley rolled to the table and joined us. Diego used a napkin for a coaster.

"My father didn't kill McDermott," he said. "No one believes me."

"I believe you," I said. "I think Tony Cedrone killed him. I think Tony killed Vincent Dunn, too. Dunn was murdered the same way McDermott was, shot two times in the head. I'm investigating Dunn but McDermott's name keeps coming up."

Diego sniffed the coffee. His face relaxed.

"They bribed my father to admit he killed Red, or at least not to deny the charges." He drank some. "He told his lawyer, that clown LaPaz, not to fight it, either."

We kept quiet and listened.

"He was terminally ill and wanted my mother to have some money." Diego shrugged his narrow shoulders. "He died in prison. No compassionate leave for nobodies like him."

"Who paid him off?" I asked.

"I don't know." He put the cup on the napkin. "I'm glad I don't know, because if I knew I'd feel obliged to avenge his death. I don't need that kind of pressure. So, if you ah—"

"So if I find out who bribed him, I'll keep it to myself."

"Thanks," he said. "My wife is expecting a boy. She's due in two months. I'm naming him Vegas after my dad."

"Nice gesture," I said.

"It's something, I guess." He looked at me. "You're looking for Dunn's killer. And you think the same man who killed Dunn killed McDermott."

"That's the theory."

"I know this will sound crazy, but if you can find a way to clear my father's name." He stopped for a second. "I don't want my son growing up thinking his grandfather was a murderer."

"It probably won't happen," I said. "Much as I'd like it to."

"I'm just saying if something falls into your lap, something that clears my father's name, it would mean a lot to me and my mother. It would to put things right."

"If I find evidence that will clear your father's name, I'll act on it."

Buckley cleared his throat.

"If Dermot can prove Cedrone murdered Red McDermott

at the behest of the FBI, I will work with you to overturn your dad's conviction. It won't be easy. And if we get it overturned, we'll go after the FBI for damages and get your family some serious money."

"Don't get your hopes up," I said to Diego.

"I won't," he said. "I know how things work. My father wasn't an angel, but he wasn't a killer, either."

"Diego." Harraseeket Kid leaned forward on the table. "I wear the same coveralls. Do you fix cars?"

"I opened my own garage last year, just starting out," Diego said.

"Tow truck?"

"A clunker," he said. "I spend more time fixing the truck than I do towing cars."

Kid and Diego talked about engines and tires and brakes and suspension. Buckley and I listened. Diego got up. I stood and shook his hand.

"Tell your mother I'm sorry and that I won't bother her again." Something occurred to me. "How did you get here so fast? A broken down truck on 93 backed up traffic for miles."

"I heard about it on the radio, a truck from Alabama was stacked too high. The traffic didn't affect me. I grew up in Haverhill, but I live and work in Chelsea. I came over the Tobin."

There's an explanation for everything.

31

THE NEXT DAY I prepared myself to meet Kenny Bowen at Harvard Stadium, where we'd be pumping iron under the concrete stands. My joints screamed 'Don't do it. Make up an excuse and skip it.' My AA sponsor, Mickey Pappas, a Greek-Irish wild man, told me that pain is the pathway to peace, or something like that. I went to the car, mentally ready for the dose of pain that would be coming my way.

I retraced the route I took two days earlier, Memorial Drive to Cambridge and over the Charles to Allston-Brighton, keeping an eye on the rearview mirror. No one was following that I could see. I again parked on North Harvard Street, and I again saw Kenny waiting for me at the gate. We walked under the stands and descended the stairs to his subterranean weight room, a hell-hole of rusting iron lit by a single bulb on the end of a frayed cord.

We warmed up on the torn mats, loosening our bodies for the upcoming torture, listening to the clanging cast-iron radiators. Kenny loaded four 55-pound bumper plates onto an Olympic bar, two on each end, and said, "Romanian deadlifts, two sets of eight for a warmup. Then I'll load the bar to the hilt for the work sets."

A 265-pound warmup set?

We chalked our hands and began to lift. With each grueling rep my spine went snap, crackle, pop, and I started to question my sponsor's wisdom. Pain might be the pathway to peace, or it might be the pathway to traction.

On it went, one power exercise followed by another. Compound movements, Kenny called them, movements that involved multiple joints. After the deadlifts, we did squats, and after squats we did jerks. Whatever ever happened to toe raises and neck rotations?

We finished the workout with a grueling set of kettlebell swings, swinging kettlebells the size of Old Ironsides' cannonballs. Why do I do this stuff? To what end? When people come at me, they come at me with guns. They don't care if I can lift a draw bridge. Kenny slapped me on the back.

"I traced the license plate," he said. "The car belongs to the Slater Mill Company."

"Do they make breakfast cereal?"

"Ha, ha, ha, you're hilarious," he said. "They provide security services, cyber security and the like. The organization is made up of lawyers, former prosecutors, and ex-cops."

"Mob connections?"

"Not that I could find," he said. "Everything about Slater Mill looks legit."

"Why are they following me?"

"I don't know." He handed me a piece of paper. "A list of Slater Mill's board of directors and staff."

I browsed the sheet and one name stood out to me.

"Superintendent Hanson is on the board?"

"I noticed that, too," Kenny said.

I thought back to the night I ran into Hanson and his wife at the Hotel Abruzzi, the night I had asked him about Captain Leo Raymond. Hanson said he never heard of Raymond and wanted to know why I asked. I told him that Raymond said that he, Hanson, had recommended me for the Dunn case. Hanson cracked that he wouldn't recommend me for anything, but I think he believed me.

"There must be fifty names on the list," I said. "Hanson could be a coincidence."

"That's possible," Kenny said. "I looked into Lieutenant Chuck Spear. He's a cop's cop, as the cops like to say. Of course, a cop's cop, carries with it a certain amount of ambiguity. Spear could be a cop who turns a blind eye to questionable things, or he could be a cop who's first through the door."

"Usually it's both."

"I did some research," Kenny said. "In Spear's case he was first one through the door, and he has the commendations to prove it. Spear is one hundred percent solid."

"An honest cop, I suppose that counts for something."

"The intrigue grows," Kenny said.

"Along with the confusion."

"You'll figure it out. You always do." He wiped his shorn head with a dry towel and put on a heavy Dartmouth sweatshirt and a black watch cap. "Let's walk around the track and flush out the lactic acid."

"Okay." I zipped up my coat and pulled on the hood. "Let's walk clockwise, so I feel like I'm making progress."

Kenny laughed. He seems to be the only one who gets my jokes. Must be his Ivy League education.

I had in my possession the Middlesex County murder book on Red McDermott, courtesy of Lt. Chuck Spear; the FBI murder book on Red, courtesy of U.S. Attorney Maddy Savitz; the FBI-Nashua Police murder book on Vincent Dunn, courtesy of Mac Woo and Remy Vachon; and the crime reports that Captain Leo Raymond gave me, courtesy of a man who lied to me. In other words, I had homework to do.

That night I went back to the hotel and read and read and read, reading until the sun rose over the expressway, reading until the noontime Angelus bells pealed at the cathedral. I fell asleep at one and slept till nine, drank a cup of coffee and read everything again. If there were dots to connect, I couldn't connect them. I fell asleep at two and slept till dawn.

32

AFTER DOWNING A pepper-and-egg sandwich at the hotel trattoria, I drove to my uncle Glooscap's garage in Andrew Square and found him in his usual spot, sitting behind his oak desk. He nodded to me, lit his bulldog pipe, and puffed until the tobacco glowed. When you're in the presence of Glooscap, everything slows down.

He invited me to sit on the couch and asked me what was on my mind. I said murder was on my mind, and I told him in detail about the murder case. I should say cases: Red McDermott's and Vincent Dunn's. I told him that I wanted to nail Tony Cedrone and Dez Barry and anyone who was involved with the murders.

He listened attentively and said, "You have little chance of bringing Anthony Cedrone to justice. You have no chance at Desmond Barry and the FBI."

"Thanks for the encouragement."

"You have uncovered a great deal of information, Dermot, but it is inconclusive. You do not have the glue that binds the pieces together into concrete evidence."

"You have to admit there's a lot there."

"There *is* a lot there, but you need to show cause and effect. Correlation is not necessarily causation."

"I flunked logic."

He dragged on the pipe and inhaled the smoke deeply into his lungs and shot two gray funnels through his nostrils. The funnels matched the color of his long pewter hair. Most pipe smokers don't inhale. They puff. Glooscap wanted to get his money's worth.

"I have known Desmond Barry's father for many years," he said. "We were ironworkers in the same union. I got to know Desmond, too. He is not a killer. A crook, yes, but not a killer. In my opinion he did not murder Vincent Dunn. Desmond is not capable of it."

Dez Barry was more than capable of killing, but I wouldn't argue with Glooscap, my father's half-brother and a cherished tribal elder. I let it go.

"I have everything there is to have on the murders," I said. "I have all the reports, and I can't do anything with them. I have the backing of law-enforcement, and I can't make use of them. I'm stuck."

"You need a different angle," he said.

"What do you mean?"

"Think about it," he said. "Your friends in New Hampshire, Mac Woo and Remy Vachon, they could not build a prosecutable case on the Dunn murder."

"The FBI took it away from them before they had the chance," I said.

"Twenty years ago, Middlesex County could not convict Anthony Cedrone on the Red McDermott murder. Somebody paid Vegas DePena to take the fall."

"The FBI essentially took the case from them, too."

"Both Middlesex County and the Nashua police had what you have, and they could not crack the cases. What makes you think that you can figure it out?"

"I have *all* the pieces," I said. "They only had the pieces specific to their agencies."

"The agencies you mentioned share information with each other," he said. "They have weekly conference calls to discuss such crimes. They must know that Edmund O'Dwyer and James Graham are corrupt. They must know that Anthony Cedrone is their henchman, and yet they still cannot bring them down. With all their resources and all their influence, they have never brought a case against O'Dwyer, Graham, or Cedrone."

Was I being arrogant to think I could do it? Glooscap wasn't finished.

"You need a different angle."

"What angle?" I asked.

"A new angle."

"I wasn't so hot in geometry, either."

"But you are good at digging."

When Glooscap speaks he never uses contractions, jargon, or vulgarities. He never utters two words when one will do. He imparts wisdom, concise and cogent wisdom. His message is simple and yet sweeping. He shifted subjects.

"How are the Alcoholics Anonymous meetings going?" he asked.

"Good, I love them."

"And the Twelve Steps?"

"Pretty good."

"You are revved up today, terribly revved up," he said. "I suggest we meditate for twenty minutes. Is that okay with you?"

"Okay with me."

He put his smoldering pipe in the ashtray.

"Close your eyes and slowly breathe," he said.

I closed my eyes and quieted my mind and slowed my racing thoughts. In the distance I heard traffic sounds from the expressway. I heard a commuter train click-clacking on the tracks. My mind downshifted. It no longer revved. The outside sounds went someplace else. I stayed this way for what seemed a long time. Glooscap tapped his pipe on his desk, signaling twenty minutes. I opened my eyes. Glooscap blew on the pipe stem, sending embers into the air like a mini volcano.

"Your father's image came to me during the meditation. He was wearing his Marine Corps combat gear, which morphed into his Marine Corp dress blues with the Silver Star on the lapel. At the end of the meditation he stood as a Micmac chief. He was holding the Micmac Grand Counsel flag, our white flag with a red cross, a red crescent moon, and a red star. His face was radiant."

"He came to me, too," I said. "We were at Red McDermott's funeral in Lowell. An Irish priest in green vestments was saying the Our Father with a Belfast brogue. Around my father's neck was a Micmac wampum belt made of whelk shells."

"Who says there isn't a collective unconscious?"

In AA we say there is no such thing as a coincidence.

Glooscap thumbed fresh tobacco into the bowl and sniffed it, picked up a box of Ohio Blue Tip Matches and gave it a shake. Plenty left. I waited for him to light up. I loved the sound of a wooden match striking flint.

"I'd like to see my father's footlocker and duffel bag again," I said. "I want to look at the old pictures."

"I shall join you."

We climbed the ladder to the mezzanine level. Glooscap unlocked the box. I saw the same items I saw the first time: family photos, my birth certificate, and so on. I unbuckled the duffel bag and took out the thermos and heard a sloshing sound. Sloshing? Was it the same liquid from the day my father died. I unscrewed the cup-cap and then the stopper and took a whiff, expecting to smell booze. I smelled nothing. The liquid looked like water. I recapped the it and a bolt of electricity shivered my spine.

Glooscap's earlier words rang in my ears. If I wanted to solve the case, I had to find a different angle. I found it, an untried angle that I alone could pursue, with the help of others of course.

"I know what to do," I said.

"I hope it is nothing crazy, Dermot."

"The thermos," I said. "Someone might have drugged it."

He took the pipe from his mouth and arched his eyebrows.

"I never before considered that possibility. Your father was a sure-footed man with catlike balance, even when alcoholically impaired. The drugging would explain his fall, if there were drugs. I wonder if they're still detectable. Many years have passed."

"I plan to find out," I said, and took out my phone

I called my friend Kiera McKenzie, who worked in the Boston police forensics unit. I told her about the thermos and asked her if she would analyze the contents.

"That's a big ask, Dermot," she said.

"I know it is."

"Every time you call me it's for a big ask. And every time I say no to you, you manage to convince me you're working on a life-and-death case. And it's always a case you can't possibly solve without my help."

"Sometimes I'm a pain in the ass."

"Sometimes?" Kiera laughed. "Go on, Dermot. Make your argument. Why should I risk my livelihood by secretly helping you with police resources?"

I told her about my father and what I suspected.

"Did I hear you right?" she said. "You think your father was poisoned twenty years ago? And you think the liquid in the thermos will prove he was poisoned?"

"Yes and yes." I shook the thermos in my hand. I just knew it held the answer. "I need to know if my father was murdered, Kiera."

"Twenty years after the fact?" she said. "The drugs will most likely be degraded by now."

"What if they aren't degraded? That's possible, isn't it?"

"Yes, it's possible, but highly unlikely." She paused. "We've developed new technologies to analyze old evidence, similar to the evidence you are talking about. Many factors come into it. For example, was the evidence exposed to sunlight?"

"It was stored in a duffel bag. No light got in."

"Has it been exposed to pollutants."

"The liquid was sealed in an airtight thermos," I said.

"Was it frequently moved?"

"It's been in the same spot for twenty years."

"Any excessive heat or temperature fluctuations?" she asked.

"It's been in a cool spot in constant conditions."

"I'm still not sure," she said.

We went back and forth. I reasoned and begged, trying every manipulative trick I knew. She listened and remained noncommittal. I stooped lower.

"He was my father, Kiera. I need to know if he was doped."

"You are relentless." She stayed on the line. "Where is the thermos now?"

"In my uncle's garage in Southie." I gave her the address. "It's set back fifty yards from Dorchester Avenue."

"I'll find it," she said. "Leave the thermos there. Tell your uncle I'll get it later today."

"He'll be here, so will I."

"I want you to leave the garage," she said. "I don't want anyone seeing us together."

I told Glooscap that Kiera McKenzie was coming to the garage to pick up the thermos, and that she didn't want me to wait for her, fearing we'd be seen together. Glooscap assured me he'd handle the exchange. I drove to Castle Island and watched the waves slapping the causeway. Seeing the undulating water helped me to think, and it helped me to plan, and I made a plan based on an assumption.

I assumed the thermos was poisoned, proving my father was murdered. If Kiera's analysis showed otherwise, I was finished. Assuming the thermos was poisoned, I conjured a scheme to trap the bad guys. It was a ragtag scheme that was as crooked as the assholes I hoped to trap.

I called U.S. Attorney Maddy Savitz and told her my plan. After a lengthy pause, Maddy asked me to repeat it, and I did. After another lengthy pause, she asked me to repeat it again. I was losing confidence.

“That’s not a bad idea,” she said.
“I think it’s worth a try.”
“So do I.”
She told me to go for it.

33

I CALLED VINCENT Dunn's brother Tommy and told him I had a plan to bring down the heads of Boston FBI, Edmund O'Dwyer and James Graham, the men who I believed were responsible for his brother's murder. I feared he'd hang up. If he did, the plan was kaput. Tommy didn't hang up. He said he wanted to hear more. I moved ahead carefully, starting with a disclaimer.

"The plan could be dangerous," I said. "We might be butting heads with Tony Cedrone and Dez Barry."

"Fuck 'em," Tommy barked with bravado, perhaps overcompensating. "The FBI, Tony, Dez, whoever killed Vin, I want 'em caught."

I added a second disclaimer.

"My plan is sketchy at best, no guarantees. You could be putting yourself and your family at peril for nothing."

Tommy didn't reply as quickly this time. The potential danger was probably sinking into his head, the danger to his family, the danger to his life. I hadn't even told him the plan yet.

He replied in a more guarded manner, asking, "Do you think it's a good plan?"

"Maybe, maybe not," I said. "The plan is a long shot, but it's all I could come up with. I'm pretty sure my hunch about the FBI is solid—that they're crooked—but that's probably an overstatement, too."

"You don't exactly inspire confidence, Dermot."

"We have a fifty-fifty chance of pulling it off."

"A coin toss," he said. "Tell me the plan, and I'll tell you if I'll go along with it."

I told him the plan, laying it out in chronological order, going into as much detail as I could come up with. It was still a work in progress in my head. When I finished, I asked him what he thought.

"Let me see if I have it straight," Tommy said. "The Boston FBI filed a case against you with the U.S. Attorney for Massachusetts, because you were screwing around with Vin's murder investigation."

"That's right," I said.

"The U.S. Attorney is sitting on the case," he said. "Why is she sitting on it?"

"She doesn't like what's going on in the Boston FBI."

"You're gonna call the U.S. Attorney and tell her to okay the FBI's case against you."

"Which will set our plan in motion," I said. "Once the U.S. Attorney approves the FBI's request, they will come at me. They'll follow me and tap my phone and do whatever else they do. That's when we set them up."

"Like the guys in *The Sting*, we sucker 'em in."

"That's the idea," I said.

"When the Boston FBI gets the go-ahead against you, you're gonna call me and ask me to meet with you, hoping they're listening in. I'll ask you what it's about, and you'll say it's about the heist money from the armored car Vin robbed, and about Vin turning state's evidence. And I'll act shocked when you tell me that Vin turned informer."

"Right again, Tommy." I said. "I'll ask you to meet me in the Navy Yard, because I don't want to talk on the phone in case someone's listening in. That's it for the initial phone call, full stop."

"I think I understand," he said. "The next day we'll meet in the Navy Yard and talk for ten minutes. During that time, I'll make wild gestures, like I don't know what you're talking about, and then I'll walk away shaking my head like I'm pissed off."

"You got it, Tommy. That's the plan."

"The goal is to get the FBI to question me about our meeting," Tommy said.

"That's the goal, and it could be dangerous."

"And I'll tell the FBI you asked me if Vin knew someone named Collings, and I'll tell 'em you asked me if Vin mentioned anything about a safety deposit box. And when I asked you about the safety box, you got defensive."

"Perfect," I said.

"The last thing I tell 'em is you showed me a key that looked like a safety-deposit key."

"That should do it," I said. "They'll come at me with a search warrant. They'll want to get their hands on that key."

"Fifty-fifty?" Tommy laughed. "I'd have to bet against us."

"I think we can sell it because of the heist money," I said. "There's three million dollars in cash to be had."

"That's a ton'a money," Tommy said. "Maybe the FBI will get careless."

"Maybe they will."

"Count me in. I'll do it."

Yes!

"I'll call the U.S. Attorney and start the ball rolling. We'll give the FBI a day or two to get their warrants in place. Then I'll call you."

"I'll be waiting."

"One last thing," I said. "After the FBI talks to you—if they talk to you—I want you to take your family and leave town for a week. There's a hotel in Maine that my cousin owns, right on the water in Ogunquit. You can stay there for free."

I called U.S. Attorney Maddy Savitz and told her to move ahead with her part in the plan. She asked me if I was sure about it, and I lied like a bastard. I told her I was absolutely positive.

I thought I heard a muffled laugh. Maybe I should be a stand-up comic.

She said she would sign-off on the Boston FBI's case against me today, saying, "Hold onto your hat, Dermot."

I asked her about the safety deposit box, and she said that her staff would bait it with cash the next day. She also told me that Susan Pike would deliver the safety deposit key to the Hotel Abruzzi later today.

"We're using a bank in Lowell," Maddy said. "We thought it would be more believable, because Dunn knew Lowell. The serial numbers on the bills will be recorded. Cameras will be mounted inside the vault. If everything goes as planned, we'll bring them down."

"We have a chance because of the three million," I said, trying to convince myself. "Greed can blind people."

"Give the FBI two days to get their warrants in order before you move ahead with the plan. Wait two days."

"Got it, two days," I said. "How are the waves in Nantucket?"

"Choppy," she said, and hung up.

34

TWO DAYS LATER it was time to act. I drove to Charlestown and visited my usual haunts, hoping to be seen and heard, hoping the gossip mill would churn out its juicy Townie grist. The hoping was unnecessary. You can't hide in Charlestown. If you burp on Bunker Hill Street, they'll tell you what you had for lunch in City Square.

I went to Kormann & Schuhwerk's in the Navy Yard for coffee, to the Halligan Club on Main for a chat with my sponsor, to Jenny's Pizza on Medford Street for a late lunch, and to an AA meeting in Sullivan Square for sobriety. I finished the afternoon at the high school track, walking laps and doing goalpost pull-ups.

The days had gotten shorter in the late fall, especially with the changing of the clocks, and darkness came as fast as blindside blitz. A sliver crescent moon drooped over the Tobin Bridge. Southeast of the moon was the North Star. It looked lethargic tonight, flickering like a flashlight on low batteries, barely holding up its end of the Little Dipper. The lack of vitality saddened me. Some days don't end, they die and die and die. I walked back to my car.

If the FBI was following me, they were doing a hell of job of it. I didn't spot anybody, didn't sense anybody, either. Doubt overtook me, and I began to have second thoughts. Stick with the plan, I said to myself. Call Tommy Dunn and start the ruse.

I called him. The conversation rolled out just as we planned it. We talked nice and slow, so the FBI could understand us. I told Tommy I wanted to meet with him to ask him a question.

"Why don't you ask me right now?" he asked as scripted.

"I'd rather talk in person," I said. "In the Navy Yard tomorrow."

"It's gonna be freezing out tomorrow. Fuckin' wind's gonna be howling. What's the big deal? Just ask me now."

"Not over the phone," I said. "It has to do with Vincent."

"What do you mean by that?"

"I'll tell you when I see you," I said.

We agreed to meet at noon in the Charlestown Navy Yard at the Dry Dock 2 Pump House. I was banking my phone was tapped. If it wasn't, we'd be wasting our time.

At eleven-thirty in the morning I left the hotel for the Navy Yard. When I pulled in, Tommy Dunn was pacing at the pump house. Nice touch, the pacing. We shook hands and ad-libbed our schtick, no script to refer to, no dress rehearsal to fall back on, but hopefully an attentive audience of corrupt FBI agents. Tommy did a theatrical job of it, from start to finish, and punctuated the scene by stomping off at the end. After the show, which I thought went well, I drove back to the hotel and waited.

And waited.

Each day I would call Buckley Louis on our burner phones and ask him if the FBI had come to the house with a search warrant. Each day he told me they hadn't. They hadn't come to the office, either. I grew impatient.

I called Maddy Savitz, using the burner. I asked her if she heard anything from Emma Hague. Maddy told me she hadn't heard a thing.

I left my room and went to the trattoria and joined Al Barese for lunch. We ate imported Italian cold cuts on French bread with freshly sliced tomatoes and homemade mayonnaise. Who knew a sandwich could taste so good? The lunch lifted my spirits.

I was washing it down with a second cup of espresso when it happened. The FBI stormed the lobby. Agent James Graham, O'Dwyer's flunky, led the brigade. He came in like a movie star, dressed for the cover of Esquire. I looked around for cameras. I didn't see any.

I had prepared Al for the possibility of an FBI raid, and he was ready. His performance was worthy of an Oscar for Best Supporting Actor.

Graham showed Al a search warrant and told him to stay in his office. Al told him to fuck off. His brother Andy restrained him. Method acting at its best. Graham, accompanied by three agents, walked with me to my room. The agents dismantled the place while Graham watched. God forbid he lift a finger. In the top dresser drawer, they found the key to the safety deposit box. Graham grabbed it and examined it.

"What's the key go to?" he asked, with his nose up in the air. "I asked you a question, Sparhawk. What's it go to?"

"I don't know."

"What do you mean you don't know?"

"I found it," I said. "It's probably nothing."

"Where did you find it?" He came closer. "This is an FBI investigation, numb nuts. You better start cooperating or you'll be answering questions from a jail cell. Understand? Where did you find the key? Chop, chop, asshole. Start talking."

"Whatever you say." I bided my time to set up the con, to get him begging like a dog for a morsel. "I found it in a brownstone in Monument Square."

"Which brownstone?" he said. "C'mon, c'mon, tell me. I haven't got all day. Details, gimme details."

Mac Woo was right. James Graham was a moron.

"The brownstone at 77 Monument Square," I said. "Somebody tore it apart looking for something. The carpenter, who's a friend of mine, was hired to do the repairs. I went up there to talk to him about doing a job at my house. That's when I saw the key."

Graham looked at it again.

"Why didn't you leave it there?" he asked. "The key, why didn't you leave it where you found it?"

"I'm not sure why," I said, pretending to be confused. "I thought it belonged to the carpenter. I didn't want to leave it on the floor."

"Why didn't you give it to him?"

"I forgot I had it," I said. "Honest."

"You forgot you had it, but you it hid in a drawer?" He said it like he discovered something important. "I don't believe you, Sparhawk, not for a goddamn second."

"What more can I tell you, Graham? It slipped my mind."

"It's Supervisory Special Agent James Graham, asshole. Don't forget it."

"I won't make that mistake again," I said. "I apologize."

I waited like a fisherman for a tug on the line. Would Graham take the bait or would he sniff out the trap? I was banking on his stupidity. He looked at the key, turning it this way and that. He bagged it, but put the bag in his pocket, not in the evidence box. Hooked.

35

I WAS FINISHING off a hot pastrami sandwich on rye with yellow mustard at Zane's when the phone rang. It was forensics expert Kiera McKenzie. Before Kiera could get a word in, I interrupted and said we had a bad connection. I called her back on my burner phone.

"My cell phone might be tapped," I said.

"I have the results on the thermos."

I told her I wanted to discuss the findings in person. Kiera, smart, didn't ask why. She said, "Can we meet at the Arnold Arboretum? That way I can bring my girls."

"Sure, where and what time?"

"The Lars Anderson Bonsai Collection at four."

"I'll be there."

At three o'clock I got in my car and headed for the Arboretum, taking the curling road that hugged the Emerald Necklace: the Riverway to the Jamaicaway to the Arborway, one continuous road divided in to three contiguous sections. Bostonians drive it like the Grand Prix. I drove in the right lane, riding the urban rapids.

Feeling irritated by the loco motorists and needing a diversion, I turned on the jazz station to soften the assault. It backfired. The blaring trumpets bopped my ears and drummed me to the folk station, where the twanging guitars tweaked my fillings and strummed me to the sports channel, where the whining callers blitzed my nerves and kicked me off the air.

I looped the Centre Street rotary and parallel parked at the entrance to the Arboretum. Kiera McKenzie was waiting for me at the bonsai collection with her identical twin daughters, Lindsey and Loretta. They looked at me and whispered to each other and giggled. They were about eight years old and beautiful like their mother. One of them walked up to me and said, “Are you a movie star?”

“Yes, I am. I’m one of the Three Stooges.”

Kiera laughed and introduced me to her daughters. “Lindsay and Loretta, this is Mr. Sparhawk. He is a friend from Mommy’s work.”

She handed them a snack and a juice box, and they sat on a bench and opened their iPads. My movie star status had vanished.

Kiera turned me away from the twins and said, “The toxicology report came back. Your father’s thermos was laced with LSD. He must have freaked out when he ingested it.”

“Jesus.” My throat squeezed. “He was murdered.”

“I’d call it murder,” Kiera said. “The fall killed him, but the drugs caused the fall. In my book that’s murder.”

“My God.”

An unexplainable feeling came over me, a feeling of relief. I was relieved my father hadn’t committed suicide. I was relieved he hadn’t staggered off the scaffolding drunk. Death by murder carried with it a speck of dignity in comparison. The feeling of relief was replaced by a feeling of pride. Proud he was murdered? Where do these emotions come from? Dead is dead, no matter how it happens.

“It’s weird,” she said. “The thermos wasn’t among the evidence we collected that day. When I say we, I mean the forensics team at the time. The thermos wasn’t catalogued.”

“I don’t understand.”

“The first time we saw it was when you gave it to me.” She let that sink in. “Someone must have picked it up before we got there, if it was there in the first place.”

"It had to be there," I said.

"There's more," she said. "I matched fingerprints on the thermos."

"They didn't degrade?"

"You said it was in a trunk or something."

"A footlocker," I said. "Actually, a duffle bag."

"The duffel bag must have preserved them. The prints belong to a man named John Mullaney. Mullaney didn't have a criminal record twenty years ago, so his prints weren't in the system then. A moot point, because we only got the thermos yesterday."

"The name John Mullaney sounds familiar."

"Mullaney worked with your father," she said. "He was working with him the day he died. The police took his witness statement. Mullaney told them your father tripped."

"He tripped all right, day tripping." I thought about the fingerprints and what they suggested. "Union guys are usually loyal to each other. Could Mullaney have simply handed my father the thermos?"

"He could have." Kiera allowed. "But if he did, he wiped his prints off the outside. The prints we found were on the inside stopper."

"The stopper under the cup?"

"We found your prints on the thermos, too," she said. "Mullaney got careless. He forgot to wipe the stopper. I asked myself, Why would Mullaney futz with the stopper unless he was putting something into the thermos? Why did he wipe his prints off the outside of thermos if he wasn't trying to hide something?"

Kiera would make a good lawyer with her leading questions. She continued.

"Mullaney is doing life without parole at Cedar Junction for felony murder," she said. "He killed a man during a robbery."

The thermos was poisoned and John Mullaney's fingerprints were on it. And Mullaney was working with my father the day he died.

"I'm talking to Mullaney."

"I thought you'd say that." Kiera called to Lindsey and Loretta. "I have to run. The girls have homework to finish. Second grade is very demanding, right girls?" They didn't look up from their iPads. "Good luck with John Mullaney, and remember, he's in for felony murder."

We walked out of the Arboretum together and went to our cars.

I joined the rush-hour traffic on the Arborway, the third leg of the Grand Prix. My head swiveled like an owl's as cars cut me off and drivers blew horns. Get off this crazy road, I said to myself. Go someplace sane. My first choice would have been Doyle's Cafe, the legendary Irish pub in Jamaica Plain, but Doyle's had recently closed.

Another place came to me, the equally famous Pleasant Cafe, where the waitresses take no guff and the menus don't require a linguistics degree to read. I drove up Washington Street and pulled into their spacious lot and enjoyed another jewel of sanity: free parking. Before I got out to kiss the ground, I called Buckley Louis. It was good to hear his calm voice.

"How did it go with Kiera McKenzie?" he asked.

"Productive," I said. I told him about the drugged thermos and John Mullaney. "Can you call your friend in the Department of Corrections? I need a visitor's pass for Cedar Junction."

"For when, what day?"

"Tomorrow if possible," I said. "I think Mullaney killed my father."

"I'll tell my friend ASAP. He owes me one. Anything else?"

"I need background material on Mullaney, where he lived, his family, that type of thing. Find me something I can use for leverage, anything that will crack him open. I want the visit to count."

"I'm on it."

36

MASSACHUSETTS CORRECTIONAL INSTITUTE–CEDAR Junction, formerly MCI Walpole, is a maximum security prison that houses the commonwealth's deadliest criminals. The prison's most notorious convict was Albert DeSalvo, the Boston Strangler, who was stabbed to death by a fellow inmate in 1973. It wasn't the rapes and murders that got him killed, but his propensity to torture animals. That's where the inmate drew the line.

At the center of the prison is Our Lady of the Ransom Chapel, which was erected by Richard Cardinal Cushing, Archbishop of Boston, right around the time DeSalvo was strangling his thirteen victims. I wondered if Albert went in for absolution.

The visiting area was similar to others I'd been in, depressing and iron-clad secure, with a soundtrack of clanging doors and buzzing locks. There was no *Shawshank Redemption* opera music piped in, no Figaro for the lifers.

A female corrections officer, a powerfully built woman who looked like she'd breeze through a Kenny Bowen Romanian deadlift workout without breaking a sweat, hoofed me across the room to a bulletproof window with a two-way phone.

"Sit here," she said, pointing to a chair. "Mullaney'll be out shortly."

Moments later an affable-looking man sat across from me. He had floppy white hair and plenty of it. The man smiled. A smiling lifer? He had all his teeth and his posture was relaxed, a winner ready to seize the day. He picked up the phone and politely waited for me to speak.

"John Mullaney?" I asked. "My name is Dermot Sparhawk."

"I know who you are, and I am indeed John Mullaney," he said. "Our persuasive warden urged me to see you. You must have powerful connections."

"My friend has connections."

I couldn't believe Mullaney was in for life. He came across as upbeat and approachable. Maybe he read *Man's Search for Meaning*. He was making the best of a brutal situation, the way Viktor Frankl did in a concentration camp.

"You knew my father," I said to him. "You washed windows together."

"Yes, yes." He nodded vigorously. "I knew him from the ironworkers, too. I also worked with your uncle."

"Glooscap?"

"A very good man, Glooscap, and I loved your father. We made a lot of money with the ironworkers, working overtime and holidays, but we blew it. Not Glooscap, your father and I. Both of us lost our jobs, fired, which is almost impossible in that union. With your old man it was booze, with me it was gambling."

"The booze I can understand, but gambling?"

"When armed goons show up at a worksite, the foreman gets antsy." He switched the phone to his other ear. "I lost everything. It was my own fault."

A prisoner admitting he's wrong?

"I want to ask you about my father," I said.

"Ask away, young man." His smile broadened. "I'm all ears."

Was Mullaney for real?

"On the day he fell, you were working with him," I said.

"Yes, I was up there on the building with him. I saw him fall, too. It was an awful sight, seeing your father hit the sidewalk. I'll never forget the thud when he landed, the shock of it. And watching him hang in midair, like it was happening in slow motion."

"His thermos was spiked with LSD," I said.

"I don't know anything about that. I never did drugs."

"Neither did my father," I said. "Your fingerprints were on the thermos stopper."

Mullaney pushed back from the window. I thought he might leave.

"Say that again?"

"I asked about your fingerprints," I said.

"Is that why you're here, because my prints were on the thermos?" He leaned forward and smiled. "The prints don't mean anything. Your father and I shared stuff all the time. All of us did. We'd say things like hand me the lunchbox, or pass me the blowtorch, or punch me out when you leave, because I'm going to the track to bet on a hot tip. We took care of each other."

"Your prints weren't on the outside of the thermos, John. They were on the inside, on the stopper under the cup-cap, which was screwed on." I let it seep in. "Your prints would have been on the outside if you handed him the thermos."

"Maybe the thermos got dirty and your father wiped it off."

"You messed with the stopper." I gripped the phone tighter, setting my knuckles pink. "I think you doped it."

"What are you accusing me of?"

"Accessory to murder," I said. "I want to know why you did it, and I want to know who put you up to it. I want to know everything that happened that day."

"I'm finished here, Sparhawk."

I figured it would go this way. Time to play the trump card.

"You're sentenced to life without parole," I said. "Maybe I can help you."

"Help me how?" He stayed on the phone. "Are you going to get me a cushier mattress? A friendlier murderer for a cellmate?"

"I was thinking about your family on the outside," I said. "I was thinking about your wife and your son."

"Watch your step."

"Your wife needs help, John. She's eight months behind on the rent and facing eviction. In a week she'll be on the street. Your son Sean is in South Bay, finishing up twenty months. He'll need legal help when he gets out."

"You know more about my family than I do," he said.

"Maybe you should try calling them."

"They won't take my calls." He stared at me. "You'll help them?"

"Tell me what happened the day my father died and I'll help them." I paused like a salesman before making a pitch. "I'll pay the eight months of arrears on your wife's rent, which will keep her out of a shelter, and then I'll pay her rent for a year in advance."

"What?"

"I talked to her landlord. He's holding off on eviction until I call him later today."

"He's holding off?" Mullaney scoffed. "The guy's an asshole—that's what I heard. Why should I believe him, or you?"

"Let me finish," I said. "Your son gets out on parole next month. My partner is a top criminal lawyer. He knows all the players in the probation department. He can get Sean the best deal possible."

"Why should I believe you?"

"I'm not finished." I held up a thousand dollar money order, playing to his self-centeredness. "I'll deposit this check into your canteen fund if you talk to me. That should keep you in M&Ms for a few months."

"Two thousand bucks?" Mullaney scratched his freshly shaven face with recently clipped fingernails. "Too bad we can't smoke anymore." He put the phone on the counter and clutched it again. "I could get killed for talking to you. These guys you're asking about don't fool around."

"I know that."

"They can get to me in here," he said. "You're asking a lot for two grand."

"Think about your wife's rent and your son's future."

"Those two don't even talk to me," he griped. "Talk about disloyal, I made one mistake and they dumped me."

"Take a minute and think it over," I said. "I need your answer before I leave."

I looked around the visiting area and saw a roomful of broken souls, probably the result of seeds sown on rocky ground. I counted my blessings. I could leave after the visit and go to the Hotel Abruzzi for a feast in the trattoria. I could slurp pasta fazool and listen to Dean Martin croon *That's Amore.*

"I didn't set a very good example for Sean," he said, interrupting my thoughts. "He's not a bad kid, takes after his mother. He got in with the wrong crowd, the oldest story in the city. My wife did the best she could with him. She put up with a lot of crap, my crap. I'd hate to see her end up in a shelter."

"I can help them both."

"I've been conned before," he said. "I've had guys promise me things they don't deliver. For all I know, somebody sent you here to see how much I'd say. The way the warden made me talk to you, I'm starting to wonder what's going on."

"I think I understand. You're talking about trust."

"I am." His face came up. "It must sound funny coming from a con, wanting trust."

"The trust goes both ways," I said. "You could accept my offer and feed me a pile of nothing. I'm as skeptical as you are."

His intelligent eyes blinked. He hadn't considered my side of it.

"What do you propose?" he said.

I'd never negotiated with a lifer before. I went with my gut.

"I tell you my theory about what happened the day my father died. Nod if I'm right, shake your head if I'm wrong. You don't have to say a word. Everything comes from me."

"I'll give it a try, but it was twenty years ago," he said. "Wait a minute. I have a question for you first. Why are you looking into it now, all these years later?"

"I wasn't looking into it initially," I said. "I was looking into the murder of a Charlestown man named Vincent Dunn."

"I heard about that. They found him in a river up there in New Hampshire."

"I was investigating Dunn," I said. "I connected Dunn's murder to McDermott's murder, which led me to my father's murder."

"I forgot about Red McDermott." Mullaney smiled. "I liked him. He never sicced the bruisers on me. He could've, the money I owed him."

"Red was my father's best friend," I said. "I went to Red's funeral with my father. The next day my father died. I now know he was killed. He was killed was because Somerville was afraid Red told him certain things."

"I still say your father fell off the scaffolding," he said, and waved away his words with a sweep of his hand. "Never mind, make your case."

"It started with Red McDermott," I said. "Red worked in Lowell as a free-lance bookie, no ties to anyone. A Somerville hood named Tony Cedrone came along and tried to muscle in on his business, but Red wasn't one for partnerships, so he went to the Feds and made them an offer. He said he'd turn state's evidence against Cedrone in exchange for immunity. What Red didn't know cost him his life. Cedrone was already an FBI snitch, still is."

"Bullshit," Mullaney said. "Tony would never snitch."

"The Boston FBI, specifically Edmund O'Dwyer and James Graham, told Cedrone that Red was going to rat him out."

"No way."

"Cedrone killed Red. The Boston FBI pinned the murder on a three-time loser named Vegas DePena, but DePena had nothing to do with it."

"I don't believe you."

"I'm giving you background info," I said. "I haven't told you my theory yet."

"There's more?"

"Be patient, John. I'm about to tell you your role in all of this."

"I had nothing to do with Red's murder."

"You owed the Somerville mob a great deal of money." I made eye contact with him, which almost never happens in a prison. "Rumor has it you're not a very good gambler."

"It's not a rumor, it's a fact."

"Tony Cedrone approached you," I said. "Here's the part where you nod yes or shake your head no. Tony said that if you drugged my father's thermos, he'd forgive the debt."

His head remained as still as a statue's.

"I'm not seeking revenge, John. I only want the truth. Think about your family."

He nodded his head. I continued.

"I'll cut you some slack. You didn't know you were dumping LSD into the thermos."

"That's the truth, I didn't know. I loved your old man like a brother. Tony said he wanted to play a joke on him. He made it sound harmless, like it was saltpeter or something. I didn't know it was LSD until you told me just now. Tony said if I dumped the packet in his thermos, he'd forget about the money I owed him."

"I thought so."

I should probably hate John Mullaney, but I didn't. He was manipulated by one of the best con men in Boston history, the notorious Tony Cedrone. If Mullaney hadn't doped the thermos, somebody else would have, some other hapless fool.

"You'll still help my wife and son?" Mullaney asked.

"I gave my word."

"Even after what I said?"

"I gave my word."

Millenary relaxed.

"Are you serious about Tony being an informer?" Mullaney seemed incredulous about the possibility. "You weren't just saying that to get me to talk?"

"The Boston FBI should assign him a desk in Chelsea," I said. "O'Dwyer, Graham, and Cedrone have been raking it in for years, and it started with the killing of Red McDermott in Lowell. And now there's Vincent Dunn. I want to make it so Dunn is their last victim."

"A lofty goal," he said. "These guys are tough, Sparhawk. Try to stay alive long enough to deliver on your promise."

"I'll do my best."

Back in my car, I called a few shady characters I knew, telling them I wanted to have a word with Tony Cedrone. I could have randomly picked the names from my contacts list. Everyone I know is shady. When they asked me what it was about, I told them murder. It was a nice way to keep the calls short. One of the guys, an ex-cop, said he'd lend me his kevlar vest for my talk with Tony. Then he said never mind. Tony shoots for the head. He wasn't trying to be funny.

I drove out of the prison lot, got lost on the side streets, and ended up on Route 1 in Foxboro. I slowed down at Gillette Stadium, hoping the genius of Bill Belichick would rub off on me. How would Bill handle a killer like Tony Cedrone? A smart man would punt, but I've never been gifted with smarts. Stubbornness yes, but not smarts. I have one other gift. I hate to lose. The idea of Cedrone getting over on me sickened my stomach. I had to bring him down, but I couldn't see how.

I kept driving.

Enough of the defeatist attitude, I said to myself, enough of the impending doom. It's time to get positive. My AA sponsor would say to me, 'Name one thing for which you're grateful today and thank God for it.' I thought it over. I was grateful that Buckley Louis talked me into filing a will last year. Maybe I should add Mullaney's wife and kid as beneficiaries before it was too late.

I picked up I-95 north in Canton, and that's when Emma Hague called. She said she'd like to get together tonight if I could fit her in. I blurted 'absolutely!' in one syllable. She said she would come to the Hotel Abruzzi at midnight. She wanted to try out her new feather boa on me. Emma said this in a husky voice. In a choked voice I told her I'd be waiting. A feather boa, the gratitude list just grew. I glanced at the speedometer. I was going eighty-five and I didn't slow down until I reached the Hotel Abruzzi.

A boa had to be less painful than the handcuffs she favored.

At midnight I heard a gentle knock. I opened the door and saw Emma Hague standing in front of me wearing a maroon snorkel coat, Canada Goose of course. The fur-filled hood covered her head. In her right hand she carried an overnight bag. Was she planning to move in? It wouldn't bother me if she did.

She removed the hood and shook loose her blondish hair. She unzipped the coat and the lapels parted like theatre curtains. Underneath it I saw nothing but tanned skin and tan lines. What is it about tan lines that drive men crazy? A woman naked under a trench coat, the one cliche that never grows stale.

She came into the room and let the coat fall to the floor, opened her bag of tricks and pulled out a feather boa. I fumbled for the 'Do Not Disturb' card, slapped it on the knob, and locked the deadbolt.

When I awoke at noon, she was gone.

37

AT THREE IN the afternoon the phone rang and interrupted the Notre Dame-Boston College football game, which was being played in South Bend in front of eighty thousand Fighting Irish fans. BC had the ball on ND's five-yard line, first and goal. They broke the huddle and lined up in a spread formation. The phone rang again. I didn't pick it up. And *they* didn't pick it up. BC's quarterback threw an interception in the end zone.

A third ring. I answered it this time and heard an angry growl on the other end. Maybe he was watching the game, too.

"Sparhawk, it's Tony Cedrone. I heard you wanted to talk 'ta me."

"I have a question for you, Tony."

"Are you Alex Trebek? What's the fuckin' question?"

"It'll jog your memory," I said. "It's from twenty years ago. It's about a thermos."

"The fuck you talkin' 'bout?"

"I'm talking about my father's thermos, the one you spiked. I found it in his duffel bag and had it tested. The liquid inside it was doped. My father drank it, freaked out, and fell to his death. But you know all this."

"I don't know nuthin' about it."

"My father kept a diary," I bluffed, hoping he'd buy it. "The diary was in the bag, too. I had to get it translated. It was written in Micmac."

"You're full'a shit."

"It said you wanted him to join your crew in Somerville. When he said no, you threatened to kill him."

"I didn't threaten him. The diary doesn't prove a thing."

"My father fell ten stories," I said. "You murdered him. I know you did. I'm coming after you, Tony. I'll find a way to put you in a cage."

"You are so fuckin' stupid. I got no idea what you're talkin' about, murdering your father, not a fuckin' clue. But I have a question for you, Sparhawk. What was the FBI lookin' for?"

"What do you mean, the FBI?"

"They searched your hotel room."

Tony knew about the search.

"You're right, Tony. A team of FBI agents came with a warrant and turned the room upside down. They found a key."

"What key?"

"Remember the day you and Dez came to the food pantry?" I said. "You asked me about the brownstone at 77 Monument Square. You asked me what I was doing there."

"So?"

"So I got curious and went back up there," I said. "The carpenter was still remodeling when I went in, and I helped him take a broken door off the hinges. Taped to the bottom of it was a key. You and Dez missed it when you demolished the place."

He didn't bother denying it.

"Give me the key, Sparhawk. I'm not joking around now."

"James Graham has it," I said.

"Huh?"

"Graham has the key. He didn't put it in the evidence box, Tony. He put it in his pocket."

"Fuckin' Graham."
Tony hung up.

The ND quarterback took a knee and the Irish won the game. The leprechaun mascot waved his shillelagh like a symphony conductor. The marching band played Shake Down the Thunder from the Sky, and the fans celebrated like they won a national championship.

The phone interrupted the pageantry. It was Kenny Bowen.

"I need to talk to you, Dermot. Today, tonight, sometime very soon."

"Sounds important."

"It is most important." Kenny wasn't one for hyperbole. "A high-level person called me with a vital piece of information that pertains to the Dunn case."

"I had plans to go to Galvin's on Gallivan tonight. My friend's band is playing there."

"In Dorchester?"

"Yes," I said. "I'll be there at seven."

"See you then."

38

GALVIN'S ON GALLIVAN is a Dorchester steakhouse that serves the best porterhouse cut in Boston. The proprietor, Craig Galvin, butchers the beef and pork at his ranch in Vermont, way up by the Canadian border where the air is fresh and the water is clean. Grass-fed livestock, he once said. Another friend told me the hogs' vegetarian diet was interrupted when the body of a Sinn Fein turncoat was dumped in the pen and the big boys gobbled him up. Shillelagh-law and probably an urban myth. But as a precaution I never order pork at the G-on-G. I have enough Irish inside me already.

Craig's place is located at the top of Gallivan Boulevard, on the border of Dorchester and Mattapan, not far from the Morton Street firehouse. I parked on Woodmere and went in.

An Irish duet named Maura and Hutchie was playing 'Brennan on the Moor,' a jaunty ballad about an Irish highwayman caught and hanged in Cork. Hutchie plucked the banjo, Maura sang the words. Hutchie called out, "Any requests, Dermot?" His mother knew my mother in Belfast. Northern Ireland is a small area. Boston is a small town.

I thought about my earlier phone call with Tony Cedrone and said, "Finnegan's Wake."

A few of the patrons said hello to me as I worked my way across the dining room. Kenny was already there, sitting at a table in the rear. I pulled out a chair and joined him. In front of Kenny sat a lowball glass filled with dark malt on the rocks, probably Johnny Walker Blue. Kenny won't drink rotgut. He doesn't know what he's missing. I told the waitress I'd have coffee. She went to the kitchen.

"I met with a top official in the federal government today," he said. "He's on the law-enforcement side of things."

The waitress came back with coffee, cream, and sugar and took our food order. Kenny and I each ordered T-bone steaks with baked potatoes and string beans. Kenny continued.

"He knows people," he said. "In Washington everybody knows everybody."

"A big happy community," I said. "What did he say?"

"You won't like it." He swirled the liquor in his glass. "It has to do with Tony Cedrone. The Washington FBI offered Cedrone witness protection for testifying against the Boston FBI."

"Wow." I sat back and whistled. "Tony always lands on his feet."

"It looks that way."

"He'll testify against Edmund O'Dwyer and James Graham." I guessed. "He's been with them for decades."

"You're correct about O'Dwyer and Graham." Kenny finished his drink and raised the glass for another. The waitress went to the bar. "To use a shopworn cliché, Tony knows where the bodies are buried."

"He should," I said. "He put them there." I stopped for a moment and listened to the duet playing Finnegan's Wake. "Tony killed my father. I should say he had him killed."

"What?"

"Yup."

"How do you know that?"

"It doesn't matter. Tony is getting a deal, full immunity. The feds will give him a new identity and a clean slate."

"Tabula rasa."

"Show off." I rubbed my eyes with the heels of my hands. "I talked to Tony today. I told him I knew he killed my father."

"Oh, man. How did the conversation end?" Kenny asked.

"I told him I'd hunt him down and drag him into court and put him in prison if it was the last thing I do."

"Dermot, you need protection. Tony is a murderer. If he thinks you're going to sabotage his deal with the feds, he'll kill you. I told you to keep Harraseeket Kid close by."

"You did."

"Call him now. Tell him what's going on."

"I'll call him tomorrow, Kenny," I said. "Relax, everything's going to be fine."

"Sometimes you can be very frustrating to deal with, Dermot."

"So I've heard."

The waitress delivered the meals along with Kenny's refill, giving us a break from a nasty topic. Five minutes later Craig Galvin came to the table and asked us if the steaks were up to par. Craig is a big man with black hair and blues eyes. He was wearing a Kelly green polo shirt with gold script that said Old Court Cork. I told Craig the steak was excellent. I didn't want to end up in the hog pen as dessert.

"There's more," Kenny said. "And you won't like this one, either. Cedrone's handler is Emma Hague."

"What?" Why didn't I see it? "When? How long?"

"I'm not sure."

I grabbed the steak knife and carved the meat and devoured a mouthful.

"If Tony has a deal in place, Emma's been handling him for a pretty long time," I said.

"I agree." He averted his eyes as if he felt sorry for me. "She's probably been working with Tony for months."

Duped again by Emma Hague. I knew from the start that her job came first. I knew she befriended me to advance her career. What was the boathouse meeting all about? Emma was already working with Tony Cedrone at that time. Maybe she duped Maddy Savitz, too.

"You never really know what's going on with a woman like Emma, do you, Kenny?"

"Nope."

Back at the Hotel Abruzzi I lay atop my bed and thought about Tony Cedrone. Would Tony tell Dez about the Judas key bagged by James Graham? If he did, Graham would have himself a mammoth headache to deal with, one that might end with a mammoth beating.

My eyelids floated down like puffs blown from a dandelion stem. A strong gale whipped the wooden window frames and rattled the puttied panes. Each time they rattled I opened my eyes expecting to see Tony Cedrone's nose pressed against the glass. I was on the third floor with no outside fire escape.

I turned on the TV and watched Celtics getting trounced by LeBron and the Lakers at the Garden. The blowout made me feel better somehow. Someone else in Boston was getting spanked tonight. I stared at the screen for ten frustrating minutes and turned it off. It wasn't the same without Tommy Heinsohn handling the color commentary, which was always green.

I opened a book by Bernard Fernandez titled *Championship Rounds, Round 2*, a collection of boxing articles he wrote for the Philadelphia Daily News. I read a piece on referee Mills Lane, the third man in the ring for the Holyfield-Tyson "Bite Fight," the fight where Mike Tyson bit off a chunk of Evander Holyfield's ear. Mills deducted two points for the earlobe amputation and allowed the bout to continue. Two bites later, Mills disqualified Tyson and awarded the fight to Holyfield. A near riot ensued. Tyson fans feeling they were wronged.

My eyes went down for good this time. I slept late and stayed in bed until two. No sense rushing into the day.

39

I WALKED UP on Harrison Avenue from Union Park, where I'd attended an AA meeting in a church basement. The daylight waned and dusk claimed the city. Darkness was coming earlier and earlier as we neared December. I crossed Traveler Street and saw the Venuti brothers standing under a streetlamp in front of the Hotel Abruzzi, the three of them smoking cigars. Benny towered over his brothers, who weren't small guys.

"Hey," I said to my protector. "I guess your services weren't needed after all."

"You can never be too careful with these things. An ounce of prevention, that was my role here." Benny offered me a Parodi to smoke.

"Thanks." I lit the brown twig with the Bic lighter he handed me and took a puff. It was like sticking my head in a campfire. "Tony Cedrone is testifying for the Feds. He'll be leaving town soon."

Benny puffed.

"No way he's leaving," said the former heavyweight contender. "Guys like Tony don't leave town, not unless they're going to prison. Where's he gonna go, back to Italy? They wouldn't have him."

"He's getting a relocation package," I said.

"He'd go insane. Tony can't live in some podunk town with golly-gee neighbors baking blueberry muffins for him. Tony needs to live on the edge. He needs his people around him."

"He going into witness protection," I said.

"Be careful is all I'm saying." Benny dropped the cigar butt into a sewer. Embossed on the grate were the words DUMP NO POLLUTANTS. "Are you going inside?"

"Sure." I tossed my burning stogie down the same grate. Maybe the rats would enjoy an after-dinner drag. "What tonight's special?"

"Back-to-basics Italian," he said. "Sausage, peppers, and onions. The chef is cooking it—not cooking it, he used a fancier word—sautéing it. Cooks cook, chefs sauté. He's sautéing it in olive oil with minced garlic and serving it over al dente ziti and homemade marinara sauce."

I salivated.

I finished dinner and went for a walk, or as the Italians say, a *passeggiata*. Benny Venuti insisted on joining me. We strolled along the street and talked about New England fighters. Benny knew them all and fought many of them. His favorite fighter was Brockton middleweight champion Marvelous Marvin Hagler, God rest his soul.

The air was cold and the first snow of the season began to gently drift down. We continued up Harrison Avenue toward Herald Street and the Mass Pike. A car with tinted windows came toward us, slowed down and drove by us. The license plate was bent in half, making it illegible. Benny stopped and watched it. So did I. The car turned right on Traveler Street.

"Looked like an unmarked cop car," I said. "I see them in the projects."

"Maybe." He pulled his hands out of his pockets. "Maybe not. The plate was buckled, couldn't read it."

"You noticed that, too."

We resumed walking, but stopped talking. Goosebumps pimpled on my neck. Tires squealed behind us. Benny, who is just a bit smaller than I am, shoved me to the ground as a shot rang out. Benny spun and landed in the street. The car door flung and a man jumped out of the driver's side.

"Run!" Benny yelled from the street.

I legged it down an alley, heard another gunshot, didn't feel anything. The alley came out on Washington Street. I sprinted left and ducked into the alcove of an apartment building. The glass door was locked. I stood with my back against the wall. I had no means of escape and no way to defend myself.

I heard traffic, a honking horn, a distant siren. I heard my heart pounding in my ears. Maybe the shooter feared the police were coming and took off. A shoe scraped on the sidewalk. It scraped again, closer this time. Was it the shooter? Whoever he was, he was only ten feet away from me.

The traffic let up. Must be a red light farther back on Washington. The scraping shoe came nearer, no more than a yard from me now. I looked around the alcove for a way out, tried the door again, no luck. The scraping shoe inched closer. A stream of condensation floated into the alcove opening. I flattened against the wall and said a prayer to St. Anthony, patron saint of finding lost things. Find me an escape, St. Anthony. I'm dead if you don't.

My shoe hit something, an aluminum snow shovel. I quietly picked it up, held it like a hockey stick, and crouched like Marciano. The gunman jumped into the alcove opening. I drove the shovel into his throat, standing him up. He gagged and fired high. I drove it into his snout, busting open up a gusher. He stumbled backward blinking. I swung the shovel to take his head off, but his heel hit the lip of the curbstone and he fell into the bus lane. The timing couldn't have been better. A Silver Line trolley rolled over him. The double tires at the accordion middle pancaked him into the pavement. I looked down at the flattened body and then at the face. It was Tony Cedrone, crushed dead.

I got the hell out of there.

I ran back up the alley and looked for Benny Venuti. He wasn't outside, but his brothers were. They looked behind me to the alley.

"He's dead," I said to them. "Tony Cedrone is dead. Where's Benny?"

"Talk to Al," one of the Venutis said to me.

"Is he okay?" I asked.

"Al's inside."

I rushed into the lobby looking for Al Barese. He grabbed my shoulder and guided me away from the front desk to the elevator bank and said, "Be cool, Dermot. Benny will be okay."

"It was Tony Cedrone," I said. "He's dead. I—"

"Take it easy."

"Did an ambulance get Benny?"

"We don't use ambulances at the Hotel Abruzzi." Al informed me. "We have a trusted doctor in Everett. He is tending to Benny as we speak. Benny is in good hands."

40

THE NEXT DAY I opened a book titled *Larry the Stooge in the Middle*, but I wasn't in a laughing mood. I picked up the newspaper and read an article about surveillance cameras and satellite cameras and cellphone cameras and how they captured virtually everything, and how everything they captured ended up on the internet. It got me thinking. Someone would soon post footage of my shovel-swatting of Tony Cedrone.

"Might as well get it over with," I said to myself as I reclined in the hotel room. "Might as well talk to Hanson."

I got in the car to drive to police headquarters. On Albany Street I swerved to avoid an addict who stumbled off the sidewalk. On Melnea Cass Boulevard I braked before bumping a j-walking drunk. Who'd have thought that pulling into a police station would be a relief? I went into the lobby and told the desk sergeant I wanted to speak to Superintendent Hanson.

"I'd like to report an incident to him," I said.

"Superintendent Hanson is extremely busy at the moment," the sergeant replied. "I can take the report for you."

"I need to talk to Hanson in person," I said. "He knows me, Sergeant. I wouldn't push it if it wasn't important."

He made a production of clicking his pen and finding a piece of paper, letting me know I was being a pain in the ass.

"Your name?"

"Dermot Sparhawk."

"Sparhawk." He jotted it down. "What is the incident you wish to report?"

"The killing of Tony Cedrone."

"Excuse me?" I had his attention. "You said Dermot Sparhawk?"

"Yes, Sparhawk."

"Take a seat," he said.

Ten minutes later Superintendent Hanson came out to the lobby and stood in front of me with his hands in his pockets. His body language said tsk, tsk, tsk. His eyes looked at me like a disappointed school teacher.

"Follow me, Sparhawk."

I followed him through the turnstiles, wondering if I'd come out again. He took me down a long hallway to a conference room and led me inside. Sitting at the table was U.S Attorney Maddy Savitz, with her long brown hair bound in a bun. Hanson and I sat with her.

"We know you killed Tony Cedrone," Maddy said. "Superintendent Hanson and I were just discussing it when you showed up."

I braced for a lambasting, having killed the star witness, but Maddy and Hanson stayed remarkably calm. Maybe it was the spilt-milk thing. Cedrone was dead and they couldn't bring him back to life, even though Hanson thought he was the Second Coming.

"I was defending myself." I pleaded. "He came at me firing a gun."

"FBI agent James Graham is dead, too," Hanson said. "Somebody beat him to death with a baseball bat."

"Hey, I didn't kill him. I didn't even know he was dead."

"We know you didn't kill him," Maddy assured me. Hanson added, "You might not have cratered his skull, but you got him killed."

They both were right.

"We strongly suspect Dez Barry of Graham's murder," Maddy said.

"Dez swung the bat." Hanson piped in. "He killed him."

"Why do you suspect Dez?" I asked, actually sounding surprised.

Maddy folded her hands on the table.

"Before we get to that, tell me about Tony Cedrone. You talked with him on the phone recently. Our intelligence confirmed you did."

"Your intelligence being Emma Hague, Cedrone's handler," I said.

Maddy blinked. Hanson looked at her. He didn't know about Emma and Tony. Maddy leaned forward.

"Did you, by any chance, tell Cedrone about the key Graham seized from you with the search warrant?"

"I might have."

"I think you did," she said. "And I think Cedrone told Dez Barry, giving Dez motive to go after Graham. Before James Graham was killed, he was badly beaten, similar to the beating Vincent Dunn endured in Nashua."

"Dez is nothing if not consistent," I said.

"You think this is funny?" Hanson barked. "One of your stupid jokes?"

"No, I don't think it's funny or a joke," I said. "I think Dez tortured Graham for the key. When Graham gave up the key, Dez killed him. He didn't need him anymore."

Neither of them said anything, but the silence was filled with stress. Hanson groused under his breath. Maddy looked at the ceiling. She turned her face to me.

"Let's assume Dez got the key from Graham," she said. "Let's also assume that Graham tracked down the location of the safety-deposit box. We left a trail of breadcrumbs leading to the bank in Lowell. Graham had to work to figure it out, but the trail was there. So let's thirdly assume that Graham told Dez where the safety-deposit box was located."

"All three assumptions are solid," I said. "Dez beat the information out of Graham. Dez must know about the safety-deposit box in the Lowell bank. He has to know. He wouldn't have killed Graham otherwise."

"As of this morning, no one has touched the box," Maddy said.

"That's about to change," I said. "Guarantee it."

"Guarantee it?" He scoffed. "Do you think you're Joe Namath? You don't know anything about anything, Sparhawk." Hanson stood. "We're through here."

"That's it?"

"Go home!"

I gladly did as I was told. I drove back to the Hotel Abruzzi and ate a platter of veal parmigiana with red sauce, wolfing it down like a hyena. Al Barese gawked in amazement. After the meal I burped and went to bed.

41

WHAT HAPPENED NEXT was so predictable it was almost laughable. Dez Barry stepped into the trap intended for FBI racketeers James Graham and Edmund O'Dwyer. He went to the Lowell bank and entered the vaulted room with the manager, an undercover FBI woman. Dez took the key from his pocket, opened the box, and got caught. The *real* feds, the internal affairs crew from Washington DC, arrested Dez and charged him with the murder of James Graham. They later arrested Edmund O'Dwyer and charged him with some kind of a conspiracy crime.

The next day I was eating breakfast in the the trattoria, reading a newspaper article on O'Dwyer's arrest. O'Dwyer accepted a plea deal to get a lenient sentence. No surprise. I flipped to the sports page and read about the Patriots.

My phone rang. It was Kenny Bowen.

"Have you been following the O'Dwyer story?" he asked.

"Enough to know he was arrested and took a deal."

"That's the surface stuff," he said. "Remember that friend I was telling you about, the high-ranking official in the federal government?"

"You talked about him at Galvin's on Gallivan."

"He called today. O'Dwyer copped to the McDermott murder."

"Why did he admit to that?"

"The feds had him cornered on a New England drug operation with Somerville. They told him they'd indict his son if he didn't cop to McDermott. The loving father O'Dwyer caved in. He admitted he instructed Tony Cedrone to murder Red McDermott."

Why did the feds care about O'Dwyer's role in the McDermott murder? McDermott was old news. I'd have leveraged O'Dwyer on the drug operation with Cedrone and Dez, which seemed more important and more current and more newsworthy.

"What about the Dunn murder?" I asked.

"Nothing on that."

"I can't see why the FBI pushed for McDermott," I said. "I don't get it."

"None of us never get it, Dermot. The feds have their own rules of logic, and you won't find them in a math book." He riffled through some papers. "I have more. I hope you're sitting down. My high-ranking friend heard rumblings, which are now substantiated, that Emma Hague will be promoted to lead the FBI in New England."

Unbelievable.

"Emma Hague gets the corner office." I said with a chuckle. "She got what she wanted." In a weird way I was happy for her. A wacky idea came to me. What if Emma pushed O'Dwyer to plead to the McDermott murder for sentimental reasons? McDermott's murder led to my father's murder. What if she was throwing me a bone? I laughed at my romantic musings, and at my egotistical foolishness. When would I learn? "So Emma is in charge of New England."

"You have a very good friend in a very high place, Dermot."

"Yup, I do."

I thanked Kenny for the update and hung up.

I thought about Diego DePena, whose father Vegas was falsely convicted for the McDermott murder. I remembered something Buckley Louis said to me. He said that if I could prove the FBI was behind Red McDermott's murder, he could overturn Vegas's conviction and sue the FBI for damages. As it turned out I didn't have to prove a thing. Edmund O'Dwyer did that all by himself. I called Buckley and told him about O'Dwyer's plea. I thought he'd fall out of his wheelchair he was so excited. He asked for Diego's number, which I texted to him.

I then thought about Vincent Dunn, the Nashua River floater.

I had a little more work to do.

43

TOMMY DUNN DESERVED to know what happened to his brother Vincent, and so did Vincent's childhood friend Eddie Loan. I called them and asked if we could meet today. They both said yes and we agreed to meet at Houghton's Pond in the Blue Hills Reservation. Tommy Dunn's truck route from Providence to Boston was taking him that way, and he said it was an easy place to park an eighteen-wheeler. Eddie Loan said that Houghton's Pond was fine with him, too.

I arrived at the pond at three o'clock. The parking lot was almost empty, but you'd expect that on a cold November day. The only people stout enough to take a dip in this kind of weather are the L Street Brownies, who swim year-round in the ocean. To them the pond would feel like bathwater.

I turned off the engine and waited under a leafless elm. Tommy Dunn pulled in driving a Kenworth long-haul tractor. He stopped the truck in the middle of the lot. The diesel gurgled and died. Eddie Loan parked next to me in a black Lincoln Navigator. The three of us got out and said hello and walked to the edge of the pond. I picked up a flat stone and side-armed it, getting six skips. Tommy zipped his Teamsters jacket to the top. Eddie smoothed his thick brown hair.

"I know who killed Vincent and I know why," I said to them. "It's a complicated story. Some of it isn't entirely clear to me and probably never will be. I'll do my best to explain it, starting at the beginning with the torture. Dez Barry tortured Vincent to find out where he hid the heist money."

"Did Dez kill him?" Tommy Dunn asked.

"No, just the torture."

"Did Vin tell him where it was, the money?" Tommy asked.

"I don't think so," I said. "I think Tony Cedrone and the FBI grabbed the money early on. If they *did* grab it, they didn't tell Dez." A thought came to me. *If Tony and the FBI had grabbed the heist money, why would they be looking for it?* I hate logic. "Forget what I said about the money. I don't know what happened to it."

"Why was the FBI involved?" Eddie Loan asked.

"Tony Cedrone was an FBI snitch," I said.

Tommy and Eddie looked at each other, and in concert they said, "No way."

"Tony was tight with the head of the Boston FBI office, Edmund O'Dwyer. Tony was also in cahoots with O'Dwyer's second in command, James Graham."

"The name Graham sounds familiar," Tommy Dunn said.

"It should," I said. "James Graham was beaten to death at the Mystic Piers. Dez Barry tortured him and killed him."

"Was Vin beaten like that?" Tommy Dunn asked.

Sometimes I hate this job. This was one of those times.

"I am sorry to say that he was," I said. "Dez killed Graham, but he didn't kill Vincent. Cedrone killed Vincent, because Vincent was ready to turn state's evidence against him."

"Fuckin' Cedrone. I hate that prick." Tommy walked up beach ten yards and bent over with his hands on his hips. Eddie and I stayed put, giving Tommy space. He came back and said, "Vin got killed because he turned informer. I knew that would get him killed."

"Vin was an informer?" Eddie Loan asked.

"That stays between us, Eddie," Tommy Dunn said. "Agreed?"

"Sure, Tommy, no sweat. I won't say a thing."

"I live in Charlestown, and I wanna stay in Charlestown. If word got out Vin was a rat, I'd have to move."

"There's more," I said. I told them about Tony Cedrone's long-time association with the FBI, and how the FBI protected him, and how they profited from each other. "When Vincent turned informer, O'Dwyer told Cedrone to kill him."

"Are you kidding me? O'Dwyer gave Tony the okay?" Tommy Dunn asked. "What the fuck are you saying, that the FBI *okayed* it?"

"They more than okayed it," I said. "They ordered it."

"They ordered the hit?" Tommy kicked the sand. "I can't believe this. Are they arresting Tony? The honest cops, will they arrest him?"

I picked up a flinty piece of shale and let it fly. Eight skips, not bad.

"Tony is dead. He got run over by a bus."

"A bus killed Cedrone?" Eddie Loan said. "That is unbelievable. The most feared hood in the city gets whacked by a bus. What happened?"

"The official version is that Tony was accidentally hit by a bus," I said.

And then I told them unofficial version, the real story. I told them how Tony chased me down an alley shooting, and how I hid in an alcove and smacked him with a snow shovel, and how Tony tripped and landed in front of a Silver Line bus, which crushed him flat on Washington Street. I told them everything.

"Thank God you're okay," Eddie Loan said. "He would have killed you for sure."

"I'm glad the bastard's dead," Tommy Dunn added. "Good job, Dermot."

Retelling the story shook me up inside. It didn't hit me until just now that I could have been killed. Benny Venuti could have been killed. My mind froze. My arms and legs turned cold. Was I experiencing PTSD? I gathered myself.

Now it was my turn to walk away. I needed a few minutes to let go of all this talk of violence. I strolled along the water's edge and looked for a stone to skip. Five minutes later I came back to them with a flat one in my hand.

"Are you okay?" Tommy Dunn asked. "You don't look so good."

"You're gray," Eddie Loan said.

I told them I was fine. We stood on the sand and watched the murky water as the sun dipped below the pines. I threw the stone, no skips this time.

"Remember that day at Pino's Pizza?" Eddie said. "You asked me about a woman named Grace Collins. Did anything come of that?"

"I looked into it," I said. "Grace Collins had nothing to do with Vincent's murder."

"Why did you ask Eddie about her?" Tommy followed up. "You must have had a reason."

"Don't you remember?" I said to Tommy. "You told me that Dez Barry asked you about someone named Grace Collins in Monument Square."

"No he didn't."

"I thought you told me—"

"It wasn't Grace Collins he asked about," Tommy said. "It was Collings with a G at the end. Dez asked me if I knew anyone named Collings in Monument Square."

"Did you say Collings?" Eddie asked.

"That's who Dez asked about," Tommy said. "Collings with a G."

Eddie Loan picked up a rock and lobbed it into the pond, making a splash.

"I think know what's going on with Collings," he said. "Collings in Monument Square, I'm pretty sure I know what Dez was talking about."

42

EDDIE BRUSHED THE sand off his hands and said to me, "Remember when I told you that Vin and I played war when we were kids? We pretended to fight the Brits at the Battle of Bunker Hill. I told you that day at Pino's."

"I remember," I said. "You and Vincent defended the Bunker Hill obelisk in Monument Square."

Eddie shook his head and then nodded.

"I said that, yes, but I didn't explain it well enough. We defended the obelisk at the old cemetery, not at Bunker Hill."

"What cemetery?" Tommy Dunn asked.

"The Phipps Street Burying Ground," Eddie answered.

"The old one by Mishawum Park?" Tommy asked.

"That's the one," Eddie Loan said. "The cemetery is laid out like Bunker Hill, with a mini obelisk at the top. Vin and I defended the graves like they were our homes. Our favorite grave to defend was a vault in the side of the hill, the *Collings* vault. The name Collings is etched on the plate that seals it."

The three of us looked at each other.

"Do you think Vin hid the money in the vault?" Tommy Dunn asked, getting excited. "Is there any chance he stashed it there?"

"I think it is very possible, Tommy," Eddie Loan said. "Your brother Vin was a smart man. I can't think of a better hiding place."

"Eddie, you're a genius," Tommy said. "A fuckin' genius!"

"A Charlestown Einstein," I added.

"I can't believe it." Tommy smiled and leaped. "We might find the heist money."

I couldn't believe it, either. And I got excited. Time to calm things down.

"How do we handle this," I asked.

"I'll drive to the cemetery right now, before it gets completely dark," Eddie said. "I'll bring my camera with me, so if anyone asks, I'll say I'm taking pictures for the historical society. Townies know me, so no one will suspect anything. I'll get the lay of the land."

"Eddie," Tommy said. "Get some close-ups of the vault so I know what we're dealing with. Should we go tonight?"

"I say we go tonight," Eddie said.

"We'll go tonight," I said. "We'll need flashlights and tools."

"That's me," Tommy Dunn said. "I have the tools. And if Eddie can text me pictures of the vault, I'll know which tools to bring."

"The cemetery is fenced and locked," Eddie said. "But there's a gap in the fence near Rutherford Avenue. I'll go there now and send Tommy the pictures."

"What time should we meet?" Tommy asked.

"Three in the morning," Eddie said, "when no one is awake."

"We'll go at three," I said. "Let's go in one car. We'll be less conspicuous."

"I'll drive," Eddie said. "I'll pick you guys up."

We went back to our vehicles and left Houghton's Pond.

44

AT THREE O'CLOCK in the morning we got out of Eddie's Navigator in Thompson Square and walked to the section of the cemetery nearest Rutherford Avenue. Tommy Dunn and Eddie Loan were wide-eyed with anticipation, and so was I. I thought of Colonel Prescott's command at the Battle of Bunker Hill: Don't fire until you see the whites of their eyes.

Eddie led us to the gap in the fence. We squeezed through it and entered the cemetery. I was struck by the quiet. Mishawum Park was quiet, no wild parties tonight. Rutherford Avenue was quiet, no roaring trucks. Maybe that's why Eddie whispered when he said, "It took me twenty minutes to find the Collings vault. We never would have found it in the dark."

Eddie guided us through a labyrinth of gray tombstones, irregular in size and shape, like the jagged plates on the spine of a stegosaurus. We stood at a row of vaults beneath the mini obelisk. Eddie aimed his flashlight at one of them.

"There it is," Eddie Loan said, "Collings, 1700–1773."

"He missed the Battle of Bunker Hill by two years," I said. "No glory for Collings."

"I'll loosen the bolts." Tommy Dunn opened his tool bag. "I'm ready for this. When Eddie sent me the pictures, I could tell they were alloy tamper-resistant bolts."

"I wasn't a history major, but I don't think they had tamper-proof bolts at the time of American Revolution," I said.

The three of us laughed, breaking the mounting tension.

"This oughta do it," Tommy said, "a hex-head screwdriver for button-head bolts."

Tommy stayed at it for ten minutes, alternating between the top and bottom bolts. He broke the seals and unscrewed them. I pulled on the door. The rusty hinges creaked and the crypt groaned open.

Eddie Loan shined a light inside. He screamed and dropped the flashlight. "Jesus, what the hell is that?"

I picked up the flashlight and aimed it into the vault and saw the decomposed body of someone wearing a floral shirt. At first I thought it was Collings, but colonials didn't dress in Tommy Bahama.

"Gimme the flashlight," Tommy Dunn said. He bent over and stepped into the vault and came out with a duffel bag. He unzipped it and packets of hundreds spilled over the top. "Look at all that dough!"

Tommy didn't noticed the decayed body. Eddie Loan took the light from him and looked inside again. "I think that's the guy from the poker game, the guy Vin killed in the fight. He was wearing a Hawaiian shirt. Remember I told you that, Dermot? Remember I said he was wearing a Hawaiian shirt?"

"I remember, Eddie."

"Vin really killed the guy?" Tommy dropped the duffle bag. "I heard the rumors, but I never believed them. I never believed Vin was a murderer."

Emotions were rising.

"We need to get out of here, guys," I said. "Seal it up, Tommy. Make it look like nothing happened. If the name Collings hits the news, Dez Barry will hear about it. Dez might be in jail, but he has family in Charlestown. They might want in on the cash."

"We don't want that," Eddie Loan said.

"I'll seal it like new," Tommy Dunn said.

Tommy finished refitting the plate on the vault, and we grabbed the bag of money and went out through the gap in the fence. The three of us piled into Eddie Loan's Navigator. Eddie dropped the keys. His hands were shaking.

"Eddie, let me drive," I said.

"Okay, you take the wheel."

We switched seats. I drove to Rutherford Avenue and took the Tobin Bridge out of the city. No one was behind us. No one was in front of us. It was four-thirty in the morning. I continued driving onto Route 1 toward Revere.

"What do we do with the money?" Eddie asked. "I don't want to get in trouble. Do you think the bills are marked?"

"The money was embezzled from a credit union," I said. "The bills won't be marked. No one will be looking for the money now that Vincent is dead, may he rest in peace."

"You're saying the money is safe," Eddie said. "It can't be traced."

"The money's safe, and we're safe. Nobody knows a thing."

"We split it three ways?" Tommy asked from the back seat.

"Two ways, you two," I said. "I'm set with money."

Eddie turned and looked at Tommy Dunn.

"No way," Tommy said. "We split it three ways. We walked into this together, and we're walking out of it together. No regrets, no second thoughts."

We drove to Revere Beach in silence. The sun was coming up on the horizon. We were in for a bright day.

"Now what, Dermot?" Eddie asked. "How do we handle this?"

"We can divide the money in my hotel room." I suggested. "It's safe there. No one will bother us."

"Sounds good to me," Tommy said as he stretched.

"Me, too," Eddie said, yawning.

The adrenaline was wearing off. I turned the car and heading to the Hotel Abruzzi. We went to my room and divvied the money three ways.

45

I SLEPT A fitful three hours. The sound of airbrakes on Washington Street woke me up for good. I showered and shaved, got dressed, and thought about the million dollars in cash I now had. It didn't feel right keeping it. I have too much money as it is, so I decided to spread it around. I'd give a quarter million each to Harraseeket Kid, Buckley Louis, Al Barese, and Benny Venuti. They earned it. Kenny Bowen, I'd pay out of my own pocket.

My cellphone rang. It was Mac Woo. I asked him how he was doing. He hemmed and hawed, which wasn't like the eloquent Mac. I asked him if he was okay.

"I feel funny about the Nonantum boathouse meeting with Maddy and Emma," he said. "I don't want you to think." He stopped. "I want you to know that I never." He stopped again. "I really had no idea they—"

"You don't have to say it, Mac. They kept you in the dark about the Cedrone deal, too."

"I had no idea they recruited Cedrone months before the meeting. I didn't know Emma Hague was his handler. I just found out about it today, after he died, of course."

"Don't worry about it."

"I've been racking my brain trying to figure out why Maddy and Emma invited me in the first place. I couldn't help them much. As you know, I'd been relegated to in New Hampshire, out in left field. The role Maddy and Emma assigned me turned out to be a sham. They never contacted me after the meeting. I keep asking myself, Why was I there?"

"Did you come up with an answer?"

"I did," he said. "I think they invited me to make you feel more comfortable."

"It worked."

"Thanks for saying that. I thought you'd think I betrayed you."

"They duped both of us, Mac." I thought about the meeting. "I don't hold it against them. They did what they did to break up a criminal enterprise. Everybody gets whacked around in these investigations. I'd have done the same thing. They accomplished what they set out to accomplish. They brought down a crime ring."

"I guess you're right about that." He hesitated. "There's another thing I wanted to talk to you about, something on a personal level."

"I'm listening."

"I'll be retiring from the FBI soon."

"Congratulations, Mac."

"I've gone from counting days to counting minutes to counting seconds." He hesitated again. "I like the way you do things in Charlestown, you and Buckley Louis. I heard you talk about your cousin, too."

"Harraseeket Kid."

"I browsed your webpage yesterday, and I noticed that you're interviewing candidates for a paralegal position." Mac cleared his throat. "I'll just come out and ask it. Can you use a lawyer with foreign language skills? I know four Chinese dialects, including Mandarin and Cantonese. And I speak Spanish and Portuguese."

"How about pig latin?"

"Expertlyyay. If you don't want me, tell me to am-scray."

After I stopped laughing, I said, "I'll talk to Buckley. I have a feeling you can start the day after you retire."

In the hotel trattoria I sat at a table with Al Barese. He told me that Benny Venuti had suffered a nick of a wound, and that he was back at it, hitting the sandbag and running on Revere Beach. I said a silent prayer of thanks and relaxed. But then I'm always relaxed in Al's trattoria. It was more like a family dining room than a commercial enterprise. I turned to Al.

"I'll be checking out soon."

"I knew you would be," Al said. "I enjoyed having you here, and to be totally honest about it, I *really* enjoyed the action. It's amazing how the threat of death gets the juices flowing. I'm going to miss you hanging around here."

"I'll miss it, too."

"You should move in permanently," Al said, spreading his hands wide on the table. "We can easily figure out an arrangement that suits you."

"I have considered it." I got up from the table. "I hope I didn't sound presumptuous saying that, but I've thought about it."

"Presumptuous? Not at all." Al stood and shook my hand. "Where are you off to?"

"Lowell," I said. "I have one more piece of business to attend to."

"Call me if you decide to move in."

"I'll let you know."

46

I DROVE TO Lowell and parked in front of St. Patrick Church. Captain Raymond was waiting for me on McDermott's Green. He was wearing the same leather bomber jacket he wore the first time we met. I crunched up the gravel walkway to him.

"I heard you solved the Vincent Dunn case," he said. "Not officially, but you caught Tony Cedrone. Too bad he died before he faced trial."

"A terrible shame, Tony dying."

"Do I detect sarcasm?"

The church bells chimed the Angelus at twelve noon. It was an overcast day in late fall, and I removed my hat until bells pealed the last note. I fitted it back on my head and looked at Raymond.

"I saw Superintendent Hanson at the Hotel Abruzzi the night you and I met for dinner," I said. "He was coming into the hotel when you were leaving it. You walked by each other and didn't say a word."

"How did I miss him?"

"You told me that Hanson recommended me for the Dunn job. I asked Hanson about it. He said he never heard of you."

"Did he?"

"So I asked myself, Why did Captain Raymond mislead me about Hanson? Why did he hire me to investigate Vincent Dunn's murder?" I didn't wait for an answer, because it wasn't a question. "I finally figured it out. It wasn't about your good friend Vincent Dunn, was it? It was about the Boston FBI and Tony Cedrone. Dunn's murder was a means to draw me in. But it wasn't about the FBI and Tony, either. It was about my father. You thought he was murdered."

"Dermot, you have to understand—"

"You picked McDermott's Green for our first meeting, triggering the last memory I have of my father. You lied to me about Hanson, knowing I'd find out it was a lie and become suspicious of you. You wanted me to look at you, and you wanted me to look at Red McDermott, because looking at you and Red would lead me to my father."

Captain Raymond didn't say anything. I peered up at the steeple. A seagull landed on it and preened its sooty wings. Only in Lowell do lowly seagulls preen with pride. Raymond extended his hands as if to make a plea.

"No way your father lost his balance and fell."

"He didn't fall," I said. "He was murdered. I talked to the man who doped his thermos with LSD."

"Anyone I know?"

I ignored the question.

"I read the McDermott file, the truthful one from Mac Woo and Remy Vachon. Red wanted to turn state's evidence against Tony Cedrone. Red then made the fatal mistake of contacting O'Dwyer's office."

"O'Dwyer, the Boston FBI director," Raymond said.

"He wasn't director back then." *And he isn't today.* "Cedrone was a snitch. O'Dwyer was his handler. Red walked into a buzzsaw."

"I had my suspicions."

"The FBI feared that Red said things to my father. Tony Cedrone threatened a window washer to spike his thermos."

Raymond bent down and put his hands on his knees. I thought he might vomit. When he came back up he looked ten years older.

"You're a smart guy," he said.

"Not really," I said. "Why did you hire me to investigate Vincent Dunn?"

"You answered your own question. I was hoping you'd connect the dots to your father."

"Is there more?" I asked.

Raymond nodded.

"When the FBI took the Dunn case from Nashua, a faint bell rang in my head, a bell from twenty years ago when the FBI took the McDermott case from Lowell, from Middlesex County, actually. I saw the parallels. That's when I thought about your father's death."

"Tony Cedrone," I said. "He killed Red, he killed Dunn, and he killed my father." The preening seagull flapped its wings and flew from the steeple toward the rivers, flying between smokestacks and mill buildings, flying over parched canals and derelict locks. "You wanted me to find out about my father. You wanted me to know he was murdered."

"Yes."

"And if he was murdered, you wanted me to solve the case."

"Yes."

"I asked myself, Why did Captain Raymond want me to solve the case?" I pointed to a granite bench and we sat on it. "I went through my father's papers again last night and found my baptism certificate. I had two godfathers, Thomas "Red" McDermott and Leo Raymond. My given name is Dermot Raymond. I was named for you and Red."

He didn't reply.

"I remembered where I saw you before. It was at Red's funeral twenty years ago, right here on McDermott's Green. You were wearing a police uniform, and you were with a beautiful woman."

"My wife."

"My father died the next day," I said. "I was thirteen. You were my godfather. Why didn't you contact me? Red had an excuse––he was dead––but you didn't."

"It's complicated."

"Try me."

He got off the bench and turned up his shearling collar.

"I respected your father more than any man I ever met in my life. Our time in Vietnam was a big part of it." He took a step and crunched the gravel. "Your father's drinking cost him his job with the ironworkers. That's no small feat, getting fired from Local 7 for drinking. Then he disappeared. Some of us thought he went back to Nova Scotia."

"I don't remember him leaving."

"You were a toddler," he said. "Your mother called me. She didn't have any food in the house. I brought over some groceries, milk and eggs, the basics. The next week I brought more."

"I don't remember seeing you," I said.

"Like I said, you were a toddler."

"Still."

"I'd come late at night, after my shift ended." He looked at the ground. "Your mother was a proud woman. She didn't want the neighbors to know about the food. I developed feelings for her, and I sensed she had feelings for me. It was all unspoken. Neither of us acted on it." His eyes welled. "I never pursued her, and she never encouraged me, but the feelings were there. I'm sure of it. My love for her grew so strong I couldn't bear it any longer. I had to walk away."

"You didn't act on it, neither of you." I mulled it over. "Must have been hard for both of you."

"That's the truth," he said. "Eventually, your father returned home. A couple of years later I met my wife."

I thought about my Belfast mother and the endless drinking and the cirrhosis of the liver that destroyed her life.

"She died young," I said.

"She did, and then your father died the day after Red, and then my wife died shortly after that, cancer."

"Sorry to hear about your wife."

"Life," he said. "I should have contacted you after your father died. I wanted to. My wife was sick, and well. I feel like I failed you. All I can say is I'm sorry."

I'd been whining. Raymond didn't deserve that.

"You walked away from my mother out of respect for my father," I said. "You don't have to apologize for anything."

I thought about my love for Cheyenne, who left me after a car intended for me hit her. Collateral damage they called it. It's not collateral when the woman you love is the one who's damaged.

"I always thought Jeepster Hennessy was my godfather," I said.

"Jeepster stepped in for Red at the christening. Red was away at the time."

"Federal prison?"

"State, Concord. He was working his way up the ladder."

A cold wind bent the trees surrounding the church grounds. A boy in a tee shirt sped by on a skateboard. Probably a project kid, he didn't notice the cold. I reached into my pocket and pulled out a packet of Effie's Oatcakes and gave one to Raymond.

"Mmm, these are good," he said.

My ears were freezing and my nose was runny. I wanted to get warm.

"I'm going to Athenian Corner for a bite to eat," I said. "Do you want to join me?"

"I'd like that."

Acknowledgements

MY WIFE, MARIBETH, who encouraged me from the first page to the last. Her feel for story is instinctive and correct. I no longer debate her when she questions the necessity of a scene. I simply delete it. I've finally learned my lesson. An old writer's adage says 'Kill your darlings,' that is, get rid of the digressions that flatten the story arc, usually ego-centric nonsense that attempts to show the reader how smart the writer is. Maribeth has perfected the art of killing darlings. She guns them down as soon as I type them into the manuscript. I must have a tell, she finds them so quickly. Not one of my novels would have been published without her keen eye and pitch-perfect ear, and her love and support.

Dick Murphy. A big part of story development takes place before a word is ever written. On a weekly basis, Dick and I discuss the plausibility of plot lines and story ideas, usually over a cheeseburger platter and a bowl(s) of popcorn at the Ninety-Nine. We talk about scenes and settings and characters and story logic. Are the ideas credible? Will the readers buy them? Once the manuscript is done, Dick dives into the actual editing, bringing to it his life experience growing up in Charlestown. E.g. 'The door splintered when I kicked it in.' Dick: 'The doors in the projects are metal.'

Dennis Hanson. Dennis knows the territorial nature of law-enforcement agencies and the sparring that takes place between them. If possession is nine tenths of the law, jurisdiction is a ten tenths of law enforcement. The begrudging cooperation that takes place between departments can add intrigue to a story, especially when you bring informants into it. Dennis spells out the best ways to take advantage of shifting departmental stances. He is also a master wordsmith, an ace grammar man, and a born editor.

Chris Hobin. An expert on dialogue flow, Chris dissects each exchange and offers pointed critiques on dialogue logic and believability. He begins with the general and drills down to the specific—word choices. He uses his Dorchester smarts to suss out the baloney that's clogging up the works. Would Character A really reply to Character B in such a way? Would he really use those words? Chris has generously edited all five of my books.

Frank Carney. I almost felt guilty giving Uncle Frank the manuscript after four rounds of editing, let alone the dozens of rewrites I'd done myself. What could he possible add? The answer: plenty. A week after I gave him the manuscript he came back with four pages of corrections and suggestions, all of which were put into play. E.g. 'Your place needs a complete do-over, cellar to attack.' Uncle Frank: 'Did you mean attic?' His insights were outstanding, exceeded only by his Irish sense of humor.

Eddie Loan. Eddie shared his expertise on Charlestown history, everything from neighborhood lore to the Battle of Bunker Hill. Eddie knows where the bodies are buried, literally. He showed me how to sneak into the Phipps Burying Ground, bypassing the locked gate, to get a firsthand feel for the setting of one of the scenes.

Sioux Gerow. Editor of the Charlestown Patriot-Bridge and a talented artist, Sioux designed the book cover, finding the perfect lettering and background to suit the story. She then worked with the formatter to get the dimensions right. Thank you for sharing your gifts, Sioux!

Patricia MacDonald. My mother put her Regis College education to work, adding the final touches to the prose, smoothing the rough edges and readying the manuscript for submission. A lifelong grammarian (a talent that wasn't passed on), she parsed each sentence for accuracy and proper word usage.

I'd also like to thank Al Barese, Andy Barese, Don DeRosa, Benny Venuti, the Panagiotopoulos family in Lowell who gave permission to use Athenian Corner, Paul Wahlberg in Hingham for permission to use Alma Nove, Craig Galvin in Dorchester for Galvin's on Gallivan, Roy Solomon for Zane's, Allan F. MacIsaac Construction, Joan MacIsaac and Irene Costello for Effie's Oatcakes, Peter Pappas, Paul "Hutchie" Hutchinson, Kenny Bowen, Sharon Hanson, John Mullaney, Lou and Kathy Certuse, Kiera McKenzie, Lindsay and Loretta McKenzie.

Made in the USA
Middletown, DE
10 October 2022

12311610R10135